No Home for My Heart

No Home for My Heart

KAREN ROSSI

A Karen Rossi Romance

Wisteria Publications

Wisteria Publications
507-4 Briar Hill Heights
New Tecumseth, ON
L9R 1Z7

No Home for My Heart
ISBN: 978-0-9735152-2-0
Copyright © 2017 by Kaarina Brooks

Published in Canada 2017

Layout and Cover Art by Taria van Weesenbeek

Please contact the author at brooks.kaarina@gmail.com for any questions or comments.

Dedication

Dedicated to the women who are struggling in a relationship with an addicted loved one.

May your story have a happy ending.

Other Books by Karen Rossi

Acknowledgements

I want to thank Taria van Weesenbeek who has given so generously of her time to bring this novel to life.

Chapter One

As soon as they stepped into the silent house, Marshall Kenton threw her black jacket on the deacon's bench in the hall and kicked off her patent leather heels. The TV weatherman had lied. The late April afternoon had turned out to be exhaustingly hot and humid.

Jonathan loosened his tie, marched straight into the kitchen and reached in the fridge for a beer. "Mom, I don't know whether to tell you or not, but—" He pulled off the tab and took a hefty gulp. "I saw Dad in church."

Marshall refused to let her face reveal the fact that her stomach suddenly lurched up to her throat and the pulse at her temples started to hammer so loudly it surprised her that her son didn't hear. A picture of calm, she walked into the adjoining family room and began to rearrange two perfectly poised flowers in one of the many bouquets that covered most of the available surface areas.

She willed her voice not to wobble, and even managed to sound bright and interested. "Is that right? Funny I didn't see him. Where was he?" An

Oscar-worthy performance.

"At the back of the church." Jonathan followed her into the family room.

Marshall turned to look at her son. A tall, slightly-built young man, he wasn't as muscular as his father was in his prime. And his hair was light brown like hers, instead of dark, like Robert's. But his eyes were identical to his father's—deep, dark blue—and they never failed to give her a jolt when they were aimed at her. Like now.

"He left just before the service was over." Jonathan flopped down on the maroon leather couch, nimbly keeping his beer from spilling.

"Did I hear you say Daddy was in the church?" Olivia came out of the hall powder room, smoothing down her navy blue skirt. "I can't believe you didn't say something to me." She cast an accusing frown at her brother.

Marshall detected the longing in her daughter's voice and the all-too-familiar twinge of guilt tweaked at her heart.

"Sure. And have you jump up and down screeching in the middle of the funeral service," Jonathan retorted.

Marshall smiled. The squabbling made it sound like Jonathan had never left home.

"I guess I wouldn't even have recognized him," Olivia admitted wistfully.

"Yes, fourteen years is a long time." With a deep sigh Marshall sank into the couch beside Jonathan and lifted her feet onto the glass coffee table. "Honey, please pour me a glass of wine. There's some left in the fridge in the bottle I opened yesterday."

She leaned her head against her son's shoulder and

Jonathan gently fluffed her reddish blond hair. "Nice hair color, Mom," he quipped.

"Thanks. Does the job."

"I still think the red is too brazen," Olivia opined. She took a sip from the wine glass she was carrying along with a tumbler of cranberry juice. "You should try a nice soft brown to hide the gray. I think that's more suitable at your age."

"Later, Sweetie. I'm too tired right this minute." Marshall accepted the stemmed glass and took a grateful gulp of the dry red.

Olivia seated herself on the rug in front of the couch and rubbed her cheek against Marshall's arm. "I should've opened you a new bottle, Mom. That wine is probably turning."

"It can't be turning. I just opened it yesterday." Marshall knew she wasn't going to win this one, but gave it a half-hearted try.

"You weren't home yesterday, Mom," Jonathan put in. "You were at Auntie Raelyn's, arranging the funeral, remember?"

"Okay. The day before then. What does it matter? I'm not that fussy about my wine."

"Wi-no!" Olivia laughed. "Next thing you'll be guzzling some kind of rotgut plonk."

Marshall tried to force a smile, but the little joke swiped just a tad too close.

"Robert, what on earth have you been drinking? You smell like the bottom of a distiller's barrel."

"Just some of that god-awful cheap wine you keep bottling. I told you it's not worth the money you think you're saving."

"I don't smell like that when I drink it."

"Sure you do. You just can't smell yourself."

It's that damned whiskey he buys on the sly. He thinks she doesn't know, but who could miss the bulge on the left side of his jacket whenever he comes home from work. It tears her heart out to see him sneaking around like a thief, trying to hide his drinking.

But she can't bring herself to tell him how ridiculously obvious his charade is. Would it help to point out he isn't fooling anyone when he comes home, clutching his jacket and holding his arm in a weird angle in an effort to hide the bulge? It would only make him embarrassed and that would lead to a burst of defensive fury and days of silent treatment.

Of course Olivia wouldn't know about any of that, because Marshall had been careful never to bring up Robert's drinking problem over the years. Not in her daughter's presence, anyway. Jonathan knew, being eight years older, but was considerate enough not to spoil his little sister's gilded memory of their father. Olivia had been only two when they separated, and as far as she knew it had been caused by "irreconcilable differences".

Which was true. Robert hadn't been willing to give up his drinking, and she'd had her fill of looking at him, listening to him, smelling him, trying to discuss family issues—or anything—logically with a drunken husband. Irreconcilable differences, all right.

The soft chirping of goldfinches at the backyard feeders drifted into the house, the only sound to break the silence of the late Sunday afternoon. Mom would never hear that sound again, lying in her coffin. Had the gravediggers already lowered it to the ground and covered it with earth? "Earth to earth. Dust to dust." What was it like to lie in a coffin? It wasn't like anything. Mom was dead.

Just like her marriage to Robert. Dead. All those dreams about "tottering down the hill together" hand in hand, like John Anderson and his love. Till death do us part. All that had turned to dust. It had been hard to give up on that dream and to let go of everything she'd counted on. But the hardest thing had been to convince herself the wonderful guy she had married was as good as dead.

She and Jonathan are walking to the park. They pass the swings and the monkey bars and head toward the far end of the park.

"Why did you bring the little shovel, Mom? You gonna build a sand castle or something?"

"I'm just going to dig a little hole over there under the trees. I want to bury something."

"What?"

"A memory."

Jonathan laughs. "You can't bury a memory!"

"It's in this little box, see?" She shows him the blue velvet jewelry box, but not its contents. They're too precious for other eyes to see.

Jonathan broke into her thoughts. "I guess Dad wanted to be there for his ex-mother-in-law's funeral."

"I can understand that. He and my Mom always got along really well."

"So how come you and Dad didn't?" Olivia asked. For the hundredth time.

"It's a totally different ballgame being married to someone." Marshall didn't embellish the statement. She was too tired to go there. "But I think we should be reminiscing about your grandma now. Don't you think that would be appropriate?" And maybe get Olivia off the subject of her father.

Olivia immediately took up the challenge. "Yes, I

think she was a very nice Grandma before she got Alzheimer's. Of course the last few years she wasn't really much of . . . of anything."

"Lots of people at the funeral said it's a blessing she's gone," Jonathan added. "You spent so much time running back and forth to Riverwood Manor the last three years. It's going to be much easier on you now, Mom."

"Yes, Mom," Olivia agreed. "Don't you think it's better she's finally out of her misery?"

Marshall's eyes filled. It was *her mother* they'd just buried and were now blithely writing off as a demented old bag. She didn't want to shoot the kids down too harshly since they were only trying to be kind, but—

"I want you to know, both of you," she said firmly, "it's *never* better to lose a loved one. It may be easier for me now, but it's not better. I'd gladly have continued to go to Riverwood after school for years and years, rather than lose her." She swallowed. "Remember that."

"But she was just a vegetab—" Olivia began, but now Marshall cut her off sharply.

"She was *my mother!*"

Jonathan gently stroked her hair.

"Please remember that." Marshall's voice wobbled. "She was my mommy."

"It's all right," Jonathan whispered. "We know you loved her. Just like we love you."

"And love never dies," Olivia recited piously.

Marshall hiccupped a sob mixed with a chuckle.

"Robert, I can't go on like this. I feel like I'm walking on quicksand. I can't rely on you any more, never knowing what's going to happen next with you. With us."

"Face it, you just don't love me any more." His words are slurred, thick and unpleasant.

"You're right. I don't." What a liar she is.

"Maybe you never did, for all I know."

Of course he is only trying to convince himself that she's been lying all along, so he can use that to defend himself whenever necessary.

"I did love you, Robert. Very much."

"You did?" He smirks bitterly. "And you're the one who always maintained your love would never die."

"I was wrong."

But she had lied. Her love hadn't died. It was Robert who had died—the Robert she'd married. Losing him had been heartbreaking.

Was it better now? She had to keep telling herself it was.

"We'll always take care of you, Mom," Olivia went on. "Even when you get Alzheimer's."

Marshall gave her daughter's flaxen head a loving pat. "God forbid. But thank you, just the same."

Jonathan tried to get the conversation back on track. "Grandma was a fun person," he said. "We played baseball and, boy, when she connected, that ball flew right over the house." He swung a high arc with his hand.

Olivia laughed. "And once it broke a window. Remember? My bedroom." She jumped up. "How about something to eat?" She disappeared into the kitchen and Marshall could hear her foraging in the fridge.

Marshall patted her stomach. "Not for me, thanks. I ate too much at the reception. The caterers prepared so much food I think we could've fed another 125 people."

"That's okay. The leftovers will feed me for the next

several weeks," Jonathan said. "You don't know how much I appreciate them."

"Oh, but I do know! And you certainly can have them, because Olivia and I are trying to eat more fruits and veggies instead of sandwiches and goodies. Aren't we, dear?"

Olivia, who had just appeared holding a cupcake, did a quick u-turn and returned with an apple.

"Those leftovers would be an unnecessary temptation for us," Marshall said. "Right, darling?"

With her mouth full of apple, Olivia nodded.

"Mom, with your figure, I don't know why you worry," Jonathan said.

Marshall laughed. "A son isn't supposed to notice his mother's figure. But thank you just the same for the compliment."

Olivia nodded emphatically. "Mom, you're in great shape for a woman your age. All my friends say so. Let's face it, a person looking at your figure would never guess you're going to be fifty on your next birthday."

"I didn't realize I was the talk of Northmount High."

They are lying in bed and his hand is stroking the bend of her ribcage, sliding down to her waist and along the curve of her hip.

With bouncing Harpo Marx eyebrows Robert murmurs his appreciation. "Darling, you're the sexiest woman in Canada."

"Only in Canada? Not the whole world?"

"I've only had experience with all the women in Canada." He heaves her on top of him, between his naked legs.

"I don't know why I married such an inexperienced man. I should have been more choosy."

He takes one of her nipples in his mouth and fondled the other with his hand, while she settles herself more snugly between his thighs.

"My friends are all jealous of me, you know. You're the sexiest wife around."

"We're supposed to be talking about Grandma, not my figure," Marshall snapped angrily and cursed silently when she saw her children's surprised faces.

Damn him! He was still causing problems. Or at least his memory was.

The moment Marshall walked into the staff room at recess break the following morning, Kelly O'Reilly, who taught in the classroom next to her, waved a floral delivery in front of her nose.

"Marsh, Marsh! Who sent you these bee-oo-tiful flowers? I'll bet they're from Steve," she cooed.

"I haven't a clue." Marshall took the bouquet from Kelly. "Maybe they're sympathy flowers from someone." She unwrapped the triangular package and a card fell out. The writing on the envelope sent a jolt of lightning through her.

Kelly eyed the bouquet with interest. "They don't look like sympathy flowers. To me, lovely coral roses spell 'suitor' with a capital S."

Without opening it, Marshall tucked the envelope into the pocket of her pants and went to get a vase from the cupboard above the sink. "No, they're not from Steve. Or from any suitor, either, so you can stop weaving imaginary scenarios in your busy little mind." She turned on the faucet full force.

Kelly picked up a pair of primary scissors from the table and snipped a corner off the packet of cut flower food. She handed it to Marshall. "So, who're they from?"

Marshall placed the vase on the long lunchroom table. "Oh, just an old friend. Someone you don't know." Kelly was right. It definitely did not look like a sympathy arrangement, but why else would Robert send her flowers? She was dying to read the card, but didn't want her friend to witness any emotions the message might conjure up.

"How do you know it's an old friend?" Kelly persisted. "You didn't even open the envelope."

"I recognize the handwriting. It's a very old friend."

In the bathroom, Marshall finally had a chance to look at the note in Robert's strong handwriting, the way it used to be before it became scrawly and almost illegible.

"You looked a hundred times more beautiful than these flowers, when I saw you in church."

No signature. It didn't need one. But what was the man up to? They'd had no contact for fourteen years, except for a few moments in the divorce court, and here he was, suddenly sending her flowers. Maybe he was out of money, and after exhausting all other avenues he was getting set to hit her for a loan. But why now? In all the years, with some of them probably spent living under bridges, he surely must have been out of money countless times. Yet he'd never tried to approach her before.

Sending expensive flowers before hitting her for a loan didn't seem logical. But then, why? She left the flowers in the staff room, rather than take them home. She didn't want to face Olivia's probing questions.

Because she didn't have any answers.

"What did your father look like when you saw him in church?"

"He looked okay," came Jonathan's terse reply over the phone.

"Did he?" Marshall took a sip from the wine glass she was carrying as she paced the family room.

"Yes. Kind of like his old self. You know, like in those old photos you have." Jonathan didn't sound overly keen to talk about it.

"Did he?" She took another sip.

"He wore a dark suit and a tie. What else do you want to know?"

"Hey beautiful, come and help me with this damned tie! Whose idea was it to have men wear them anyway? Must've been a woman."

"Of course it was a woman. How better to yank you guys around? Or would you prefer a nose ring?"

"Baby, you can yank me around by something else much more effectively. You wanna feel? It's getting ready for a yank."

"Stop being disrespectful. We're going to Great-uncle Fred's funeral."

"Great-uncle Fred wouldn't have minded. He used to like a roll in the hay as much as the next fellow. Ow! Not so tight!"

"Well, stop talking like that about my uncle."

"Like what? He was a horny old bastard and proud of it. Ouch!"

"Tighter! Tighter!"

Marshall chuckled into the phone.

"What's so funny, Mom?" Jonathan asked.

"Just a memory. Your father didn't like ties."

"That's funny? I don't like ties myself."

Marshall sat down on the couch, carefully balancing

the phone and her drink. That was another thing about Jonathan that reminded her of Robert. "So he looked healthy and clean?" But was he sober?

"Healthy? Yeah, I guess I'd have to say he was. Tanned, with a short, trim beard. You know, not a bushy one."

She'd always liked his beard. "And tanned, you say?"

In the divorce court, Marshall feels sick to her stomach. Robert, sickly pale, with an unkempt beard and disheveled hair. His clothes, probably from the Sally Ann because they certainly aren't his own. His outfits used to be carefully selected from the best men's wear stores. He's probably pawned those off long ago.

His eyes—his dark blue eyes, the most gorgeous eyes in the whole world, and not just in Canada— beseech her to change her mind. And, though she's promised herself she won't look at him, of course her undisciplined head turns in his direction. She sees his lips form the soundless words as clearly as though he'd shouted them.

"Please, don't do this."

It takes every ounce of willpower to force herself to turn away and not rush to him, take him in her arms and stop him from hurting. She knows he is aching inside, because so is she. It is in her power to heal his hurt, but that wouldn't solve anything. It would only be a Band-aid on a huge problem that requires aggressive surgery. How often has she fallen into that trap over the years.

But it is now finally, irrevocably over. The judge pronounces the divorce as final.

Marshall gripped the phone and squeezed her eyes tight in a futile attempt to push the memory away.

Tears filled her eyes and she held the phone away from her, so Jonathan wouldn't hear her sobs.

"Mom?" she heard him call. "Mom! Are you there?"

"Of course I am. Don't panic. I was just blowing my nose."

"So are you going to do anything?"

"About . . .?" What was Jonathan getting at? With the back of her hand, she wiped away the tears from her cheeks.

"About him."

Astonished, Marshall almost dropped the phone. "What kind of a question is that, for Pete's sake? I'm not going to do *anything* about him. We've been divorced for nine years. I have no idea what he's been up to all that time. And I don't want to know. He came down for my mother's funeral. Period. End of story."

But why had she called Jonathan to ask about him?

A huge floral arrangement waited on the front steps when Marshall got home from school the next day. She glanced around, as though expecting Robert to jump out from behind a juniper bush. Surprise! Because she knew the flowers were from him. Of course someone could have sent a late sympathy arrangement, but somehow she just knew they were from Robert.

Inside, she set the flowers on the deacon's bench and, with hands that were far from steady, she opened the enclosed envelope.

"*To my beauty.*"

Bitter anger coursed through her. She dropped the card and clenched her fists to prevent them from shaking. What, in the name of all that was holy, was the man doing? Was he out of his mind? Having DTs again? Although the handwriting looked too firm and steady for a drunk to have scribbled the words.

"Marshall, my little darling, you're sho beautiful and I love you sho mush." His words are slurred. His eyes red and bleary. The single rose he holds out to her shakes in his hand. *"For you,"* he says with a drunken grin that sends shivers of revulsion and anger through her.

"But it makes me sho sad that you're unfaith-hic-ful to me. It makes me sho, sho sad." The droopy-dog eyes try to focus, and then change to slits of evil suspicion. Angrily he throws away the flower. *"Every guy is after you. I don't—hic—like that!"*

Cold fingers of fear rub away the disgust and put her on her guard. He can be dangerous in this delirious state.

She hurries off to get Olivia from her crib, and again takes the children to the neighbor's for the night.

A motel room for her. Again.

Fear now raised waves of nausea in her stomach. Was Robert stalking her? Somehow that didn't seem likely, not after all these years. But damn it all, those kinds of things happened. Dead, estranged wives and girlfriends grabbed too many headlines, although that usually happened shortly after a separation.

But still . . .

Marshall snagged the bouquet and marched out the sliding doors to the back deck and stuffed the whole arrangement into the compost bin. With an involuntary shudder, she wiped her hands on her thighs and quickly returned inside, locking the door after her.

This couldn't be happening to her. Not now. She'd already lived through hell after telling him she wanted a divorce and ordering him to move out. Marshall gave a mirthless snort at the memory. Robert move out voluntarily? Not in this lifetime!

"This is my house!" Thunderous curses follow the declaration. "No way are you going to throw me out of my home."

"I wasn't going to—"

"Well, I'm not moving, so get that through your head! And I'm not signing any papers!"

"The court will have something to say about that."

"Yeah, so you can live here with your boyfriend. The jerk I saw you with the other day."

She sighs with resignation. "You must have been hallucinating. I've never been with any jerk. Except you."

"You're calling me a jerk? You bitch! Whore!"

Marshall shook her head at her incredible stupidity. What an asinine thing it had been to call him names. Of course it had only led to more aggression, a night in the motel for her, and another "fun sleep-over" for Olivia and Jonathan at the neighbor's house. What would she have done without wonderful Ann next door!

Chapter Two

"Robert!"

The man at the door thrust a box of chocolates toward her, but Marshall stood in shock, a stormy wave frozen in time.

"May I come in?"

He was, just as Jonathan had described him, a picture of health. Tanned, with a short, trim beard, except that instead of the dark suit and tie, he wore jeans and a light spring jacket. One detail Jonathan had failed to mention, but which she immediately noted, was that there were streaks of gray at his temples. And the lines on his face were deeper, which only made him more handsome in a mature, virile way. Of course Jonathan wouldn't have been looking at his father like that.

And, Lord help her, neither should she!

"May I come in, Marshall?"

She blinked at the sound of her name and moved aside to let him enter. It was an automatic gesture of politeness which she immediately regretted. This was not wise. But there he was now, standing in the foyer, looking around him with obvious interest.

"I see you kept the deacon's bench I made you for Christmas." His voice was still smooth and low. She'd always loved to hear it over the phone. And in the bedroom.

She must not allow her mind to wander to such places.

Her mouth was so dry she didn't dare attempt a reply. Why hadn't she just told him to say his piece standing out on the steps? Too late now. She licked her lips to moisten them.

"What are you doing here?" Marshall was thankful the words didn't come out as a croak, and she crossed her arms, striking a defiant, unwelcoming pose. She left the door open, hoping he would take the hint and leave before he saw through her bluff. Because she was definitely not feeling brave. And she didn't think even whistling a happy tune would help.

"I have something I need to say to you."

Damn it! The man seemed to totally ignore her show of insolence.

"You haven't heard of the telephone?" She tried to sound churlish. "A great invention. Been around for a few years now."

"I figured you'd probably hang up on me."

"Ah, a brilliant deduction."

"I also wanted to see you."

He didn't make a move to come any closer, but furtively Marshall began to sidle toward the family room, where the sliding doors led to the back yard. It was almost instinctive, for she'd always had to have an escape route available, just in case he became violent.

"So you've seen me. Now say what you have to say

and then get out." It was totally out of character for her to be this rude, but exceptional circumstances called for exceptional measures.

He stepped toward her, holding out the box. "Chocolates. Dark, with Maraschino cherries."

He remembered, damn him. "No thank you. I'm on a diet," she snapped.

Robert smiled and placed the box on a small table by the wall. "You sure don't look like you need to be. Maybe Olivia will like them."

"Olivia? As in your daughter? Whom you haven't seen in fourteen years? That one?" Marshall's voice rose higher and higher, ending up in a squeak.

"Yes."

She could tell from his low, even reply that he wasn't going to start defending himself. But his Adam's apple worked, and she knew that inside he wasn't as collected as he wanted her to believe. Funny, how even now there was very little they could hide from each other. He probably knew exactly how she was feeling, too, which made her feel very vulnerable, standing there in front of him.

"What do you want?" That was perhaps not the smartest thing to say, considering she didn't give a tinker's damn what he wanted. And it could lead to a conversation.

"What I want is . . ." He appeared to be searching for the right words, perhaps uncertain how they would be received. "I want my wife back," he finally blurted out belligerently.

Despite herself, Marshall drew in a quick breath of surprise. Of all the things she might have expected him to say, this was definitely not even close.

Marshall took several steps back, bumped against

the leather couch and stopped. Forcing her voice to be as firm and cold as possible, she replied, "You're crazy! I'm not your wife. Haven't been for nine years. Or technically it's fourteen, counting the separation. And that is the way it's going to remain."

She was relieved that Robert didn't try to close the space between them.

"I expected you to say that," he replied. "But I'm really sick of living my life without you and I want to have you back."

"Are you insane?" His outrageous words helped Marshall gather up the courage to stand up to her full five foot seven and look him squarely in the eyes. "I hope you don't think I'm being rude—" Oh, go ahead and think so, she couldn't care less. "But I'm really not interested in how sick you are of your life. I happen to be totally content with mine. I went through hell to get rid of you and there's no way on God's green earth I'm going to go back there. For you to even think of such nonsense goes to show how alcohol has addled your brain."

Robert remained calm, which was very uncharacteristic for him, and totally unexpected. "I know how incredibly absurd this all must sound to you, but please believe me when I say that things are different with me now. When I saw you at Nora's funeral, I knew I had to try and get you back. I know we have a chance to make it."

A high-pitched, incredulous laugh burst out of her. The man was mad! "You *know*? You know we have a chance to make it? My God! What could possibly make you *know* that?" Her frenzied heartbeats threatened to cut off her breathing. "This is so unbelievably ridiculous I can't believe I'm hearing it. But just so you know, let me tell you that my life is peaceful and organized and just the way I like it. I have no intention of jumping back into that inferno, thank you very much."

"This time it won't be like that, I promise you, Marshall." His outstretched palm appealed for her to believe him. "I need you."

He is standing at her bedroom door in his navy pajama bottoms, his dark hair tousled, looking like a sad little boy. But his words are not those of a child.

"Marshall, I need you. Please come and lie with me and let me hold you."

"Go away, Robert. Don't come into my room." She has to keep her words curt and firm. She can't let him see how this is tearing her apart.

"I have such an awful pain gnawing at my chest. I know if I could hold you for just a little while, it would go away. Please?"

"No, Robert. Go away."

"I promise I won't do anything. I just want to hold you against me."

"No. Let me sleep."

Slowly he turns. She can hear his bed squeak slightly in the next room as he settles down on it.

Then her tears begin to flow and, she knows, so do his.

She fought to take in some air. If she hadn't been clutching the back of the couch, her legs would have given out from under her. Violent, invasive emotions raged inside her. The man who, for fourteen long years, had been as good as dead to her, had just appeared, very much alive, and was trying to thrust himself back into her life.

And churn her inside-out in the process.

As the tidal wave inside her settled down to mere raging surf, she was able to breathe again. Shaking her head, she croaked, "Robert, just go. Please."

She didn't want to hurt him. He looked so earnest, it was cruel to slap him down. But she didn't ever want to deal with that pain again. Ever.

Please, don't do this.

Marshall shut her eyes. No! Not again! Every time she relived that scene in the divorce court, she felt a stab of pain and pity for that disheveled, unkempt man who used to be her handsome husband. She knew alcoholism was an illness, but he refused to get help, and she'd had to ensure her own survival as well as that of their children. It wasn't because she didn't love him any more. Never that.

But, looking at him now, she could plainly see he was a totally different man from that poor wretch in the court room. Was it really possible he had overcome it?

"Things are going really well for me," he said, as if in answer to her thoughts. "I've been sober for nine years now." There was a touch of pride in his voice.

Aren't you pleased with me? Like a little boy. Well, she wasn't going to fall for it.

"I have a construction company. Doing great," he continued.

"I'm happy for you, Robert." *Please don't tell me any more. I don't want to know anything about you. I don't want to feel anything for you.*

Marshall would have given anything to be able to sit down and take the weight off her wobbly legs, but she didn't want to give Robert the wrong signal. He might think she was inviting him to stay.

If only she could tell him to get out—now—before

she began to feel again. "Get out, Robert!" What was so difficult about saying that? But somehow the words were stuck inside her and refused to come out.

He really did look the way he used to, years ago. The way he always looked now when he came to visit her dreams and made love to her. And she would wake up in an empty bed, her loins pulsing and her heart beating madly.

"Marshall, I've missed you." Robert took one step toward her. "I've missed you so desperately all these years."

She did not want to hear that. She wished she had another pair of hands to clamp over her ears. This pair was needed for clasping the back of the couch behind her to keep her from collapsing.

"Sometimes I dream you're lying beside me. I wake up so happy and I reach out for you—but you're not there."

The anguish in his words finally made Marshall find her voice. "Stop it!" she cried. "I don't want to hear about your damned dreams. I don't want to hear anything about you."

"Marshall, I—" He took another step forward.

"Leave!" she screamed. "Get out right now!" Her stomach convulsed, and she lunged for the box of chocolates on the table. "And take your damned chocolates with you!"

Seething with uncontrollable fury she flung the box at him. "I would rather choke than eat them, and Olivia doesn't want them, either!"

He didn't dodge or make a move to protect himself. The box hit him square on his broad chest and fell to the floor, breaking open. The contents scattered across the floor and onto the oriental carpet.

"Don't you dare pick them up!" she screeched when he made a move to bend down. "Just go! Now!"

He turned and walked out through the still-open door without a word, but not before she had glimpsed his eyes. *Please, don't do this.*

She ran to the door and slammed it shut behind him and then, sobbing uncontrollably, she fell onto her hands and knees and groped blindly for the candies. Tears streamed down her face and she brushed them off with fingers, sticky with chocolate.

Damn him! And damn her for letting him in. Not just into her house, but into her awareness, into her life, back into her heart.

Although that was one place he'd never left. Despite the years of her pretending he was dead, he'd remained lodged deep in a small crevice of her heart and, much as she'd tried, she'd never been able to evict him.

Marshall thanked her lucky stars that Olivia wasn't home to pick up the mail, or there would have been some quick explaining to do. As she slowly made her way up the walk, shuffling through the envelopes, she came to a dead halt. A letter addressed to her in the familiar, strong handwriting stood out from among the usual crop of bills. It had the return address of a downtown hotel—a luxury chain she never would have stayed at herself, not on her teacher's paycheck.

As if that was supposed to impress her! With a scornful snort, she unlocked the front door and entered the quiet house. Amber wasn't there to greet her, wagging her bushy tail. The dog hadn't been there for five years now, but Marshall still missed the greeting. Faithful old Amber had slept with her master's slipper between her paws till she died. They'd buried the worn slipper with her.

Without opening it, Marshall tossed the envelope into the rattan wastebasket by the deacon's bench and headed for the kitchen to start dinner.

She was not the least bit interested in anything Robert might have to say. She took out a defrosted filet of lake trout from the fridge and went out to the back deck to fire up the barbeque. Olivia would be home from school in half an hour or so and—damn! She might look into the waste basket, see the unopened letter and pick it up, thinking it had fallen there by mistake. She was curious about everything, and she would never let an envelope remain unopened, even if it was just an advertisement.

Having lit the barbeque, Marshall hurried back to the entrance hall and fished the letter out of the waste basket. She couldn't deny that her own curiosity was piqued almost to a breaking point. But not quite. She would only slit it open and then toss it back, making it look like discarded junk mail. The wooden letter opener hung on a hook by the hall mirror and, with a shaking hand, she reached for it.

She wasn't going to look, but even before the envelope was fully open, she knew the battle was lost. She drew out the crisp hotel stationery and unfolded it, while her heart hammered in her ears.

My darling Marshall,

I know seeing me again after all these years was a shock.

To put it mildly.

I'm sorry I didn't take it more slowly and wait a few days before coming to see you in person, but I really didn't have any plan of action in mind and was flying by the seat of my pants. Or rather by the commands of my heart.

Don't say things like that. Just don't.

It was never my intention to meet with you when I came down to Toronto. I was only going to attend Nora's funeral service and then drive back home, but as I told you the other day, seeing you in church made me change my mind. When I went back to my hotel room afterwards and lay there, thinking about you—about us—I knew I had to at least make an effort to convince you that we can make it together. I know we can! Like I said to you, things are different now.

Hah! How many times had she heard that line before?

I've been sober for nine years now. I'll admit that for five years after the separation I plunged all the way to rock bottom and found myself sleeping on the streets and at the Sally Ann. I did try to join AA for a while, but when I kept falling off the wagon, I stopped going.

It was when I saw you the last time, in the divorce court that did it for me. It finally hit home that I had lost you forever. And that's when I checked myself into rehab. I'm a changed man. I hope you believe me when I say that for nine years I haven't touched a drop of alcohol.

Marshall snorted. And why should she believe him?

Marshall, I can just hear you snorting in that funny way of yours, because I know you don't believe me but it's true.

She put the letter down. Tears blurred her vision while a chuckle bubbled up from deep within her. Damn him! Did he have to know her so thoroughly?

That did it for me. I'm not the same drunken idiot I was when you finally had the smarts to call it quits. I'm only sorry you endured so many years of hell with me. You should have kicked me out years earlier, but you were always too stubborn, weren't you, Mrs. Fix-it? You honestly thought you could help me, and you didn't know when to give up. I want to tell you now that I really appreciate your efforts, even though they were futile.

Yeah, thanks a whole bunch.

As we both know, I'm the only one who could make the decision to quit drinking and to stay dry.

She wished she'd accepted that years sooner. It would've saved a lot of heartache. But then Olivia wouldn't be here. The baby had been conceived in a foolish attempt to make things better. What folly! What a stupid reason for bringing a child into the world. Marshall had known it was a failed attempt even before the baby was born.

And then, when she needed him . . .

"Jonathan, where's your father? I think the baby's coming."

She can see panic and fear in the boy's eyes. "I don't know, Mommy. Do you want me to go look for him?"

Guilt gnaws at her for putting her son in such a situation. "No, Honey. I'll phone your Aunt Raelyn. She's at work, but she'll come with me to the hospital. You can have a sleep-over at Mrs. Hall's." That wonderful Ann next door!

Marshall ran her fingers through her hair. Olivia had been a beautiful baby and now was a delightful young girl. She couldn't imagine life without her. There never were easy answers, were there?

Her eyes went back to the letter.

As I told you, I have a construction company that I established six years ago and it's doing great. I'm very proud of it. There's no lack of jobs for a carpenter in the cottage country. I have a few guys working for me and right now we're building a small shopping mall up north in Bracebridge. Whenever I have the time, I also do boat repairs. That's always been my passion, as you may recall.

Yeah, sure. She remembered all those "boat repairs" he went to do for his friends and always ended up on a binge.

I'm my own boss. The money isn't as steady as when I was a construction engineer, but I find this work much more satisfying and rewarding.

Yeah, less responsibility, he meant. No one could get killed on his watch. Marshall shook her head. That was nasty and unfair of her. Robert wasn't responsible for the unfortunate accident that had killed the worker. But since he was supervising the project, he'd taken it hard. The really serious drinking had started shortly after. But he'd always liked alcohol, so he would probably have eventually become an alcoholic even without the accident.

I've bought a sailboat and I live on it all summer. And when I'm on the lake with the sails billowing in the wind, I always dream of having you there with me. Like we used to be.

Marshall, please give us a chance. Call me and tell me you'll meet me.

Not in this lifetime, bucko! Marshall refused even to look at the phone number that followed. With her excellent memory for figures she just might remember it after just one glance.

I'll always love you.

Robert

Marshall crushed the letter in her fist and walked

with determined steps to the garage. She flipped the lid off the galvanized garbage can and buried the crumpled letter deep in the waste where Olivia would never find it.

She was not going back. End of story.

Rain was coming down in sheets when school was let out. Marshall stood inside the front doors, debating whether to make a dash for her car or wait for the downpour to end. Then she thought of the groceries she needed to pick up and decided to make a run for it. Holding a plastic bag containing her students' work over her head, she pushed open the door and rushed out into the rain.

A strong hand took her by the arm and she whirled around to face Robert.

"Let's go for a drive," he said and quickly steered her toward the parking lot. Several students were waiting for their rides under the overhang, so there was nothing for her to do but get into his waiting car without a murmur. It wouldn't have looked good for a teacher to start screaming and struggling in front of the children.

Robert drove to the main thoroughfare and headed directly south toward the lake. Up to this point, Marshall had been too shocked to speak, but now she found her voice.

"Just what the hell do you think you're doing, Robert, shanghaiing me like this? I can call the police and report you."

"I waited all week for your call and it didn't come," he told her. "I had to see you."

"I resent this kind of treatment," Marshall began, but somehow the wind had gone out of her sails.

Although her brain tried to tell her this simply was not right, on a very basic level, the woman in her found his masterful approach fascinating. This man took charge, unlike the useless drunk she'd lived with for so many years. He wanted her and was determined to have her.

The sexual attraction that had always been there between them now tried to raise its hungry head, and Marshall had to beat it down with forceful blows. No! Never again.

"Well, if you'd agreed to meet me somewhere," Robert said, and she could see the slight grin in his profile. "I wouldn't have had to resort to these caveman tactics."

Caveman. Yes, that's how he used to be, carrying her up the stairs to their bedroom while she screamed with laughter and pretended to struggle. They would almost rip off each other's clothes in their urgent need to mate, kneeling on the carpet to shed the last bits of underwear, before falling onto the floor, hungry for each other.

A shiver of desire racked her body. No! She must not remember.

"So where are you taking me? To your cave?" She hoped her sarcasm would hide the tremor in her voice.

"Not this time. I want to see the lake. Such a shame about all this wind going to waste. My boat is still up on its cradle and I miss sailing." He was silent for a moment. "You did read my letter, didn't you?"

Well, she sure hadn't intended to, but . . . "Yes."

"So you know I have a sailboat."

"Yes." You're not going to draw me into a chummy conversation, bucko.

"I really hope you'll come with me for a sail when

it's launched. I know you miss it, too."

"Forget it. I'd barf all over it," Marshall snapped. Then a dry chuckle bubbled out. "But on second thought maybe I should . . ."

The deep sound of Robert's laughter brought back memories she wanted to forget. Marshall turned her head to hide the moisture that filled her eyes. Stop laughing like that, Robert. Just cut it out.

"That's what I've missed about you," Robert said and put a hand on her knee.

She jerked her leg away from his reach. "Missed what? Me barfing all over the boat?" Although it was always he who did the barfing when he'd had too much to drink. Why couldn't she say those words out loud? Why was she being so careful not to hurt his feelings?

Robert laughed again. "Your dry sense of humor. I've missed it."

"I remember you called it sarcasm and hated it."

"I may have said that, but it wasn't true." His Adam's apple moved as he swallowed. "After the separation, I missed that about you. In fact, I've missed everything about you."

He parked the car on the high bluffs overlooking the lake. In silence they sat, while strong gusts lashed out with a fury that shook the vehicle. The wind had whipped the waters into a frenzy of foam-crested breakers that attacked the shoreline below.

Robert leaned his arms on the steering wheel and stared ahead through a windshield that was quickly becoming blurred. Raindrops ran down the side-windows in rivulets and soon they were enclosed inside a very intimate, watery cocoon.

Marshall's fingernails dug into her palms. Feelings that she'd been stomping under her feet for all these years were on the move, charging her up with a sexual tension that made the air crackle around them. Her skin prickled and she rubbed her arms. *I hope he thinks I'm just chilly.*

Robert sat up and casually placed an arm in a friendly fashion on the backrest behind her. But when his fingers lightly brushed the back of her neck, she knew he was up to something much more dangerous. The touch made her spine tingle and created a need inside her so strong she was ready to throw herself into his arms. The caress was thrilling beyond her wildest memory and it took every ounce of willpower to force herself to move away from his reach.

"Robert, what the hell are you trying to do?" she hissed, crushing herself against the door.

"What do you think?"

But he didn't try to reach for her again and she almost cried out, wanting him to touch her. Instead he placed his hand on the gearshift knob.

"I think you're way out of line, mister!" Marshall ground out through her teeth.

"What did it feel like?"

A little smile played on his lips. Oh yes, she remembered that smile. The one that used to precede sex. The smile that showed he was sure of his power over her and confident of what would follow.

The arrogant bastard thought he was irresistible. "It felt like shit," she spat out. "Don't touch me again." *Please do!*

"I could feel you trembling. You want me." But his hand stayed where it was.

She couldn't help staring at his strong fingers, the way they caressed the smooth knob. Desire rose in her mouth and she swallowed. "It was a shiver of revulsion you felt."

It was getting very difficult to keep lying to him, with her body screaming for him. *Please, just this once! Then never again. I promise.* The urgency was almost unbearable.

"I can tell the difference," Robert said with unnerving calmness. "I remember how you reacted to my touch. To sex. And I can see the desire in your eyes. You want me as much as I yearn for you." Now his hand came out to touch her arm. "Look at me."

As the savage wind shook the car, Marshall tried to stop her body from trembling with the intense need that ravaged her. But the moment she raised her head to look into his eyes, she knew she'd made a fatal mistake. His dark pupils almost hid the blue.

Like strong magnets his arms came out and pulled her against him. There was no resistance on her part and she simply melted into his embrace with a small, impatient whimper. Just before his mouth covered hers, she heard the groan from deep inside him, like from a drowning man who, at the last moment, had grasped a life ring.

Chapter Three

And then his lips were on hers, crushing and hungry. There was nothing gentle in the way he forced her mouth open and thrust his tongue inside, but it was no more violent than her own reaction. Gasping with arousal, she pushed herself against him as their tongues sparred in a fury of foreplay. Her fingers buried in his hair, pulling him closer—closer still.

Robert stopped his caressing and his fingers began to deftly undo the top buttons of her blouse. When his hand found its way inside her bra and grasped her breast, his frenzied movements stopped. A deep sigh of satisfaction told her that he now held the treasure he'd been longing for.

"Marshall, darling," he whispered. "How I've missed you. Missed this."

The nipple stood firm under his palpating fingers, eager to give satisfaction to the beloved mouth that was still too far away. How she wanted to feel the avid suction and hear his murmurs of pleasure.

Robert's other hand was now groping for her zipper, and hers went down to feel his hard erection. The thought of having it inside her almost made her weep with yearning. She rubbed her palm over it, feeling the familiar length.

"Not here," he murmured against her neck. "Darling, let's go to my hotel room."

The fatal words made Marshall sit up with a jerk. What was she doing? She wrenched herself free and backed into her corner, pulling her blouse tightly around her heaving breasts.

"No!" She uttered the word thickly, swallowing down the lust that was still pulsating through her body. "No sex. No sex," she panted. "It's not going to happen again."

Robert raked a trembling hand through his hair. "But, darling, you want it, too." His voice was pleading. "You can't deny that."

Marshall lowered her head, not wanting him to see the naked desire in her eyes. "No, I won't deny it," she quietly admitted. Then she took a deep breath and looked at him earnestly. "Robert, every time we argued, and every time I tried to leave, we made up after some hot and heavy sex. And then the cycle started all over again. We never resolved anything, because the sex always covered up the problem. But it was only a temporary respite. Yes, I admit it was good, and that's the reason it was so dangerous. So deceptive. It made us think that everything was all right with the world, just because we were in each other's arms again. But it wasn't. No matter how you promised not to drink, you always did."

He looked sullen. "I did try. I even went to a treatment centre. Please remember that."

"You don't have to remind me. After five months on the wagon you decided you could have the odd beer.

And it was downhill from there, again. And again."

"And you don't have to remind me," Robert snapped, obviously frustrated over the interrupted sex. "I know damn well what happened. But as I told you, I've been sober now for nine years and I think you could give me credit for that. It's time for us to try again."

"No, it is *not!*" Marshall shouted above the storm. "It is *never* time for us to try again. And I'm not giving you credit for nothing!"

She saw Robert's mouth open and quickly interjected before he could say anything. "I know it's a double negative! You don't have to point that out to me. *I'm* the teacher in this family."

"I didn't say nothing."

His eyes smiled and she could tell he was fighting to keep his mouth in line. This silly sparring with words made it seem like they'd never been apart, evoking memories that shot through her. She wanted those days back.

"I will not be drawn into the same old scenario again," she said firmly, defiantly.

"How can you call it the same old scenario, when I've been sober for nine years? Eh?" It was obvious that Robert was trying to control his irritation. "You could at least give us a try. Even convicts get a second chance."

"This wouldn't be a second chance. It would be . . . what? The fourth? Fifth? How many times did we separate? And then we always got back together to have wild sex."

"Who's counting?" He was annoyed, and switched on the ignition to let the wipers clear the windshield.

The storm was still lashing at the waves, pushing them toward the shore, to crash and break against the rocks. Marshall felt like she was also being forced toward some inexorable fate, to once again break against the rocks.

She shivered at the thought, but refused to get sidetracked. "*I'm* counting," she snapped. "You have no idea how disappointed I was after that five-month reprieve ended. And then there was the night you died."

"I did not die!" he yelled, slamming his palm on the steering wheel. "Why do you still keep saying that after all these years? God! It's so stupid."

"As far as I was concerned, you died." Marshall spoke with a quiet calm. The memory of that night was still as fresh and painful as when it happened. And that's when she'd finally called it quits. Forever.

"You were dead to me after that," she said. "And to keep you dead, I buried you."

Roberts jaw dropped. "What the hell are you talking about?"

"I buried you. In a tiny grave in a corner of the park where we used to take Jonathan to play."

"I don't believe I'm hearing this," Robert said with a shake of his head. "It's gruesome. Morbid. Look, I'm actually bristling." He held out his tanned arm, where the hairs stood stiff.

Marshall went on without mercy. "Remember the picture of you that I always said was my favorite? The one where we're laughing in the snow bank and you're so unbelievably handsome?"

He nodded. "So what did you do? Pricked needles into it? Ran it through a shredder?"

"No. I put it in a little box with the yellow rose you gave me on our first date. I had kept it, pressed inside my photo album."

He nodded again. "I remember. And?"

"I buried them, along with the note you slipped to me in high school, asking me for a date. I buried them all."

"You're a sick-o, Marshall."

"I had to do something to convince myself that the man I married and loved so much was gone forever." She wasn't going to cry. "The drunken slob was not the man I married. My Robert was dead."

"Okay. So maybe I was dead." Robert seemed to understand, for he no longer appeared angry. "But I'm back from the grave now." He reached out and laid his hand on her arm, causing the spot to ignite spontaneously. "Believe me, Marshall, I'm not the drunken slob any more. I'm the man you married. Older and grayer and a lot wiser, but basically the same guy." He gave a little grin. "As charming as ever."

Yes, he was as charming as ever. And Marshall had to admit he certainly looked like he was doing well. No sign of the poor wretch in the divorce court. She couldn't deny the fire that had always burned between them was still there and didn't even need a spark to ignite it. Spontaneous combustion would do it. And she loved him, as she always had, through all the horrors of alcoholism. Through all her denials of his very existence. And he still loved her and wanted her. So what was stopping her from taking him back into her life?

"I love you, Marshall," he said roughly. "As much as before. Even more, now that I know what it's like to have lost you and to be without you."

So what was stopping her?

Fear!

The storm continued to rage.

What if he started to drink again? She would kill herself, rather than go through the agony of separation again.

"Marshall?"

"Let me think about it." Was she really saying that? Was she crazy? Why was she even considering it?

With a triumphant laugh, he pulled her into his arms. "Take as long as you want, my own darling," he said and kissed her.

The heat of his embrace threatened to engulf her again, but before she went off the precipice, she pulled back, gasping for breath.

"No, Robert," she cried. "I don't want us to start like this, by falling into bed. This time—if there is going to be a this time—it has to be different."

"But, darling, that was always the best part! How in hell can you expect us to be together and not have sex? It would be cruel and unnatural. For both of us."

"Maybe. But there has to be more to us than just sex."

"*Just sex?* My dearest Marshall, most people would kill to have the kind of sex we had. And can still have."

He was right, of course, but she had to be firm. She had to. No way was she going to have things start off the same way, and be doomed to end up the same as before. Was there anything else to their relationship besides great sex? Because sex hadn't been enough. After a few weeks, sometimes just days, things had always ended up falling back to the old ways.

"Marshall, honey-bunny, come to bed." His slurred words make her shudder.

"I don't want to be in bed with you. You stink."

"Whaddya mean I shtink? I just had a shower, for chrissake!"

"The smell of alcohol is coming out of your pores. It makes me sick."

"Hey, it's just my aftershave, honey-bun." He staggers forward. *"You won't even notice it when we get —hic —goin'."*

"Keep away from me!"

His drunken titters revolt her down to the very marrow of her bones.

"Here I come, ready or not!" He lunges toward her.

Another night at the local motel. It's that, or risk being raped. Luckily Olivia and Jonathan are having a sleep-over at their grandparents'.

"I'll only consider getting back together if you agree to do it my way." She was absolutely insane to even consider it at all. Who was putting these words into her mouth?

"And that is . . .?" Somehow he knew he wouldn't like the answer.

He didn't.

"No sex." Marshall said calmly.

"No sex?" he almost yelped. "But sex always bound us together. All that time when I was grappling with my drinking, I know sex was the only thing that kept you from leaving me. And you know it was sex—pure unadulterated lust—that first attracted you to me and took us through the last year of high school."

"You make it sound so . . .so primitive," Marshall protested, but she didn't deny it because they both knew strong mutual attraction had been there right from the start. It was a simple fact.

"It was primitive," he said. "I didn't know what I was doing and neither did you. We learned together. And boy, did we learn!" He grinned, running a hand through his hair. "Talk about primitive. It was downright savage."

Marshall shook her head. "It's a wonder I didn't get pregnant sooner."

"Sure is. And you know it was sex that kept us going all the way through university, when we struggled with that god-awful long-distance relationship. It's a wonder I passed any exams. I spent my days thinking about the next time we'd meet and my nights in a sweat, missing you, wanting you so much."

His body hardened with want, just remembering how they always came together after the month-long wait. She would run to him and jump into his arms, twining her legs tight around his waist, right in front of her parents' house, in full view of any neighbors who might be watching.   And her kisses—there was nothing like them in this world or the next! Breathless, passionate, soft, yielding, biting, raging, they ran the gamut from angelic to devilish and every nuance in between.

"Somehow every niche of our bodies fits together so damn well." Robert's voice was almost a growl. "Remember those cuddles on the front seat of my car? They made my blood race." His throat tightened up, forcing him to swallow. "And the wild sex in the back seat. Remember how in cool weather, we'd have to grope our way through layers of each other's clothing to find the body parts we were dying to join."

Marshall swallowed. "I . . . I don't want to hear about it, Robert. Please stop. This is ridiculous. I already said, 'No sex'. And I meant it."

He could tell she was only trying to sound angry and he continued the assault. "The first time we spent a whole night together in your home, when your parents were away for the weekend—"

"I said stop this!"

"Lying naked in bed, clasping you against me, my heart pounding like mad with pure happiness. Our legs and arms tangled tightly around each other. I thought I'd died and gone to heaven. I couldn't wait for us to be married and lie like that every night, making love without reservations and restrictions."

"Please?" she pleaded.

He could feel her becoming softer by the minute, because even after all this time, he could still read her like a book. He tasted victory and refused to stop. "And you told me that—"

"I said stop!" she cried. Gripping the door handle she made a move to get out of the car. Her furious eyes told him she she was ready to hit the road.

Alarmed, he reached out and placed a placating hand on her arm. "I'm sorry sweetheart! I won't say another word about sex."

Marshall hesitated, her hand still on the door handle. "Promise?"

"I promise. And I'm sorry I tried to bully you into changing your mind."

He sighed with relief when she settled back into the seat. She was stubborn enough to walk home in the pouring rain if necessary, and he knew it. She'd done it before.

"Robert, let's go home now. I'll drive."

"I'm not leavin'. Frank and I are talkin'. Sh . . . stop interrupting us with your whinin'!"

"The people want to go to bed. It's two in the morning. There are no other guests left here."

"Frank and I are havin' a conver-shation. Get outta here."

"Fine. I'm leaving."

"You aren't takin' the car, dammit!"

It is New Year's Eve and no taxis are available, so she walks three miles home in the dark in her party clothes, freezing her toes and fingers.

The next morning he arrives home in a cab, as from so many other parties, in a drunken haze, deeply regretful.

Just one of the hundreds of memories that still haunted him.

"There's something we have to talk about first," Marshall said decisively after a moment's silence.

What now? Was she doing her best to make this as difficult as possible? When he'd made the decision to approach her after seeing her in church, he didn't have anything more definite in mind than to get her in bed and take it from there. Things always worked themselves out after sex. They'd always felt so warm and close toward each other afterwards, nuzzling and continuing the loving touches.

"What is it?" he asked, not able to keep the irritation from his voice. "You've nixed sex, so what other wrench are you going to throw into the stew?" He shouldn't have asked, for now she lowered the boom.

"Remember Jonathan and Olivia? The two children you sired?"

"Hey, cut the sarcasm! I'm very aware of our children. But if I'm not mistaken, they're adults now."

"You're right, and I'm sorry. The sarcasm was totally uncalled for."

"Okay, then." He nodded, grudgingly acknowledging her apology. This wasn't going the way he'd envisioned. If things had gone his way, they would be in bed by now, engrossed in fabulous sex. And instead she wanted to talk about their kids.

"Frankly, I don't have the greatest memories of Jonathan. He was a sulky, belligerent ten-year-old when I last saw him," Robert admitted. And their daddy-son relationship had been wiped out by his alcoholic rages. Finally his son had started to ignore him completely, as if he didn't exist. Which was just fine with him because then he didn't need to make any effort to be a father. He just told himself it was the kid's fault for being so sullen and unapproachable. Though he knew deep down, he'd never admitted to himself it was obviously a self-preservation tactic on Jonathan's part, to escape any more hurt.

Robert looked down at his hands on his lap, ashamed. But now it was Marshall's turn to press on.

"And Olivia?" she asked.

He hardly knew the girl. As far as he was concerned, it had been a mistake to have her.

She coos lovingly as she nurses the baby in the middle of the night.

"Just listen to you! The only one you care about is her! Doesn't anyone else in this family count except that squealing kid?"

"Yes. Jonathan does."

"What about me? Aren't I worth at least a kiss now and then?"

"No. Not when you talk like that about your own child."

"My own child! It was a huge mistake to ever have that kid. That baby's turned you into some kind of a Mother Goose. She's come between us. You don't care about me any more."

"The whiskey bottle has come between us, Robert. You love that bottle more than anyone or anything else."

"I love you more than anything else."

"No, you don't. I come second, and you know it."

"You're just refusing to work on our relationship."

Another memory he wanted to zap out of existence, but it refused to disappear. Impatiently he rapped his fingers on the dash. "So what do you want to tell me about them?"

'We can't just ignore the fact that Jonathan has no good memories of you. And Olivia doesn't have any memories of you at all. How do I . . . how do we tell them that we're . . . dating?"

He smiled. "Is that what we're going to be doing? Dating?"

"What else would you suggest we call it?"

"I guess you're right. If we can't just get into bed and carry on from there—which I still maintain is the most direct way to where we're trying to go—we'll have to do it your way."

He would've agreed to anything—stand on his head for a week if necessary—to get to his desired goal. And she wasn't making it easy, taking away his trump card. He knew exactly how to get her warmed up and eager for sex, which was obvious from what had almost happened a few moments ago. But if he tried that now, she would fold her hand and leave.

He knew she wasn't stupid. She was walking into a situation that could very well blow up in her face.

Robert chewed his knuckles. If only he knew himself that he wasn't going to blow it. But he could never be one hundred percent sure he wouldn't ever have another drink. Even when he celebrated his nine years of sobriety, and even as he cheered every successful day, that awful fear of one day falling off the wagon never left him. He knew it could happen. It had happened to others. He also knew if things didn't work out for them, he would never get another chance to try.

"So what about the kids?" Robert asked.

Marshall laughed mirthlessly. "I've no idea how they're going to react."

"So . . .?"

She sighed. "So maybe it's best not to say anything until you and I've had a chance to meet a few times. This may end up going nowhere fast, you know."

Robert's heart squeezed painfully. Not if he could help it.

"We've been separated a long time," she went on. "There's a lot of water gone under the bridge and we can't just start dating and having—" she swallowed, "fun, as though we were a couple of high school kids. I hope that's not what you envisioned when you came to see me."

Robert grimaced and shook his head. "Of course not." That's exactly what he'd envisioned. But no matter what restrictions she placed on the path, he wasn't about to change his mind. Nothing would deter him from his goal. Having been with her today, he was more determined than ever to win her back.

But how should he start? She loved flowers but right now they probably sat at the bottom of a garbage can. The box of her favorite chocolates had earned him a warm invite to vacate the premises.

He coughed. "How would you like to have dinner with me as our first date?" He felt about as confident as a boy thirty-five years his junior asking a girl out for the first time. Or maybe fifteen-year-olds these days wouldn't be nervous at all. Who knew?

Marshall smiled. "I guess that sounds as good a plan as any." Then her face became serious. "But

Robert, there's another thing we should discuss before we set any dates."

He let out an impatient puff of air. "Now what?"

"Other relationships in our lives."

He hoped she didn't notice the way his hand jerked on the steering wheel.

"What about them?" Surely she wouldn't call it quits over the few women he'd slept with over the years. "It's been a long, lonely time and I can't claim to have been celibate. I'm no monk, after all."

"True, but I don't believe in starting new relationships before breaking off old ones."

"I agree, but that's not a problem now. I'm not seeing anyone."

Her next words fell on him like the proverbial bombshell.

"I am. I first have to break up with Steve."

She had a lover! But that shouldn't surprise him. She was a beautiful, vivacious woman. Alive and sexy. He swallowed. It would have been more surprising if she didn't have a lover.

Lightning flashed and a second later came the crashing boom of thunder.

"Who's Steve?" he snapped abruptly. *I'll kill him!*

"He's my friend. My boyfriend, if you wish."

His words ground out of him. "I don't wish."

"You said yourself that you haven't been celibate. Well, neither have I."

Robert frowned at her. "But I was talking about me. You're a mother! And a teacher, for chrissake. Not a wanton woman of some kind."

Her amused laughter filled the car. "Robert, you're so funny!"

"I'm not trying to be," he muttered. "I fail to see what

you find so hilarious in this."

"Actually, I'm just flabbergasted by your reaction. It's incredible." She shook her head. "And yet, so like you."

There she was again, saying things to infuriate him. "Whaddya mean so like me?"

She pursed her lips and continued to shake her head, as if he were some dumb kid. "You could never acknowledge that what's good for the goose is also good for the gander."

He slapped the steering wheel. "I could, too." What the hell was she getting at?

"When your father left your mother and took up with Sharon, you were able to deal with that, but when your mother got herself a lover, you were horrified."

"I fail to see the humor in my parents' marital problems." Robert scowled and crossed his arms across his chest.

She patted his shoulder, which irritated the hell out of him. "We won't go there, as it's obviously still a sore point."

He gave his shoulder a jerk to shake off her hand. "I was just a kid."

"Whatever. But you have to accept the reality that I have had lovers in the last fourteen years, just as you have."

"Lovers?" he almost shouted. "You've had more than one lover? Not just this . . . this Steve?" For few moments he sat, chewing his lower lip and trying to block out of his mind what her words implied. At last he sighed. "All right, if that's the way it's been."

But couldn't she have been at least a little upset about *his* lovers? How come she took it so lightly? Wasn't she jealous? He certainly was. With all these men! He was burning with jealousy.

"Well, what do you think I should have done?" she asked. "Wear my widow's weeds for the rest of my life?"

"What widow's weeds? I wasn't dead," he ground through clenched teeth. "Why are you harping on that ridiculous nonsense?"

"You were dead to me," she calmly replied. "Drowned, as a matter of fact."

"All right! Enough already!" In the small confines of the car his voice thundered loudly. "I'm sick of hearing you talk about my death. Let's settle this God-damned matter right now, while we're digging at every other issue on this planet."

He hadn't meant to make her angry, but his yelling succeeded nicely in doing just that.

Chapter Four

Marshall shrank into her corner, while the pain of that night once again dug into her like claws. Why should she go back to that black moment? Why should she even attempt to relate the incident to him again? She'd tried to explain it to him shortly after it happened, but he hadn't comprehended the horror of it all with his drink-addled brain. So what did it matter if he understood how she'd felt that night? It wouldn't change anything that had happened afterwards.

Yet, if they were going to try to rebuild their relationship, it was important to her that he finally understood how his actions had affected everything in their lives from that day on.

For a long time she sat, trying to convince herself that maybe this time he would understand what anguish she'd gone through that night. Now that he was sober, maybe he would see why she'd called it quits. She stared at the lake through the misty windshield. The water was still gray and foamy, but the wind had almost totally died down. She was thankful Robert didn't prod her. After several failed attempts, and a lot of swallowing, she was able to begin.

"You remember the day in late August—it was a Saturday—when we decided to go to a movie with the kids after dinner?" She spoke slowly, deliberately, to make sure he grasped every word, every detail. "We thought we'd go to a drive-in, because Olivia was only two, and we figured she'd probably fall asleep and we could enjoy the show in peace. Jonathan was really looking forward to this family outing, especially since it was his first time to a drive-in. Naturally we hadn't had very many of these kinds of family events, with your drinking always getting in the way."

"Okay," Robert muttered. "We know that."

"You went sailing in the morning and the plan was that when you got back, we'd go for a hamburger and then to the movie." Marshall swallowed to lubricate her throat. It was difficult to spit out the words through a mouthful of sand. "At six you hadn't come home, so I told the kids we'd drive to the marina and wait for you on the dock. That way we could just get the burgers and drive straight to the movie. It didn't start till dusk, so there was plenty of time. I wasn't worried, but the kids were getting hungry and antsy.

"We stood on the dock, waiting for you. Olivia had on a pretty pink dress and Jonathan had combed his hair with water and put on a nice shirt, so he'd look handsome at his first drive-in movie. He was such a sweet, cute kid. You'd been sober for a month or so, and I know his hopes were high that finally you'd . . . and so were mine."

Marshall heard Robert's harsh intake of breath. It sounded like a sob. "I'm sorry," he whispered.

"Yes. So am I." Her voice was flat, expressionless.

"We sat at the end of the dock, waiting. Around seven Don Sherwin and a couple of his friends came in from their sail. You remember Don?"

Robert nodded. "Of course I remember Don. His C&C was docked beside us."

"Jonathan helped secure the lines. He was always such a keen beaver around the boat, eager to help you. Not that you ever gave him credit."

Robert winced. "I didn't know."

"Yes, I realize that." Marshall said bitterly. "You were always too drunk to pay attention to him."

"I was a lousy father."

"Yes." The word was colourless. She stared out at the lake that was getting calmer. If only she were. The memories stirred up the bottom waters of her soul into a turbulence that she wasn't sure she wanted to face again.

After a while she went on with her story. "Don asked me why we were there, all dolled up, and I told him we were going to a movie and were waiting for you. He said he'd seen you out on the lake earlier in the day, but lost track of you.

"We waited till almost eight and then I took the kids for a hamburger. I knew it would be too late to drive to the movie, so we went home. Jonathan was so disappointed, I almost cried. Olivia didn't care, of course, but it was no use trying to make excuses to Jonathan. He knew you'd just plain forgotten.

"The kids went to bed but I couldn't sleep. You'd never stayed out on the lake overnight. Never. So I kept listening for you to come home. I knew exactly what I was going to say to you when you walked in through the door and it wasn't going to be complimentary. But you didn't come. And you didn't come. By two o'clock

I was absolutely certain that something had happened to you. You had to be in trouble. You couldn't possibly stay out all night on the lake without letting me know. You just couldn't do that to someone you loved and cared about.

"I stopped seething with anger and began to fret and worry. Perhaps you'd fallen into the water, and in the dark no one could see you or hear you. At that hour, who would be out on the lake, anyway? And I knew you never wore a lifejacket."

Marshall scowled at him and then went on.

"I was frightened. In my desperation I began to pray. You know I've never been religious, but I thought if you were in the water, and if praying could help you . . . Not just crossing my fingers kind of praying but really praying from the bottom of my heart. I got out of bed and fell on my knees and I prayed and prayed. Never had I entreated God so fervently. 'Dear God, please let Robert be all right. Please don't let him be in the water. Please, dear God, please help him!'

"For another few minutes I sat in the dark on the bed and rocked back and forth in agony. There was no doubt in my mind that you were dead. I knew it. And I felt the gut-wrenching agony of losing a person I loved with all my heart and soul." Marshall's voice broke. "Because that's how I loved you."

Robert's hand came out and covered hers. "I'm so sorry," he whispered hoarsely. "I'm so awfully sorry."

"Yes. So am I." Marshall removed her hand and placed it on her lap, where her fingers curled into a fist. "But I knew I had to do something and not just lie in the dark, agonizing. I had to try to find you. So I woke up Jonathan.

"'Daddy's not back yet,' I told him. 'I'm going to see

if he's decided to spend the night on the boat.'

"I asked him to look after Olivia if she woke up before I was back, and I drove to the marina. I was hoping the boat would already be in the slip, in which case I would just return home and yell at you in the morning.

"But the slip was empty.

"You were still out there in the night," Marshall continued. "I knew you were a strong swimmer, but when it's dark, it's easy to think negatively about everything. In my mind you were in the water. Drowned.

"I drove down the highway to the police station and made a missing person report. They were sympathetic, but the Marine Rescue wouldn't be able to do anything till daylight. I knew by then it would be too late. It already was.

"'He's not wearing a life jacket,' I told them desperately, but there was nothing they could do in the middle of the night.

"I knew I wouldn't be able to sleep, so I drove back to the marina. Foolishly, instead of parking in the parking lot, I drove to the nearby beach, thinking I would have a better view of the lake while sitting in the car. That was a mistake. The wheels got stuck in the soft sand and I couldn't budge. Of course there was no one around at that hour, so I walked a mile out to the highway, hoping the service station was open. It was. A tow truck came and pulled the car out. I felt pretty foolish, especially when a police patrol car came to see why a tow truck was pulling a car out of the sand on the beach at that hour."

Robert chuckled. "That's something I could see you doing."

But Marshall didn't even crack a smile. "I knew he thought I was drunk. It would have been comical under some other circumstances. That night it was not."

Robert sobered. "I'm sorry. I didn't mean to make light of the situation."

Marshall didn't acknowledge his apology, but went on. "The constable shone his flashlight on my face. 'Let me guess,' he said. 'You decided to wash your car at three in the morning.'

"'I'm waiting for my husband,' I told him. My voice trembled and tears flowed down my cheeks. 'He's out there and I'm afraid he's fallen out of his boat. He's got a drinking problem, you see.'

"The officer apologized for his inappropriate humor and offered to wait with me till the morning broke. The air was chilly by the lake at that hour, so we sat in his patrol car, just watching the lake for any signs of a returning sailboat.

"'I'm sure your husband's all right,' he kept assuring me, but I knew he was wrong. You were dead.

"The officer's duty was over at six, but he stayed on so I could sit in the warm patrol car.

"'He's a lucky man to have a wife who loves him so much,' he said to me."

With an involuntary groan Robert put his head down in his arms on the steering wheel. His shoulders shook.

Marshall went on. "Then, as the sun came up, I saw something orange far out on the lake.

"'Is that an orange life jacket?' I cried eagerly. Maybe you were wearing one after all.

"But my hopes were dashed as the object floated closer. It was only the rising sun reflecting off a large piece of driftwood, turning it orange.

"And then, a few moments later, I saw a sail out on the horizon. I stared at it as it slowly came closer. There wasn't much of a wind, so it took forever, but finally I was able to distinguish the shape of our sailboat.

"'It's him!' I shouted and jumped out of the car. I never did thank that kind policeman who'd sat there with me, comforting me with his encouraging words and keeping me from crying in despair.

"I ran to the dock and stood, trembling, as the boat neared the slip. But as I reached out to take a hold of the bow, there you were, sitting at the helm, looking at me with your blood-shot eyes, with a drunken grin on your face. Anger, like a bolt of lightning, zapped through me. Never in my life had I felt such a strong impulse to kill. I grabbed the bow as the whole torturous night flashed before my eyes. With all my might, I pushed the boat out again, sending it floating backwards, floundering toward the other boats. You had already cut the engine, so I knew you had little control, but I couldn't have cared less.

"I didn't stay to see if you managed to avoid a collision. I turned and blindly ran to the car. Luckily it was early Sunday morning, for otherwise I don't think I would have got home without an accident. Every fibre in my body was convulsed and shaking with fury. How could you have put me through this agony? How dared you look at me with those blood-shot eyes and grin at me like a drunken idiot?"

Robert jaw clenched and his Adam's apple worked.

"Luckily Jonathan and Olivia were still sleeping when I arrived home, because I couldn't stop shaking. I slipped into bed, pulled the duvet over me, and lay there, curled up, whimpering. I was sure I was bleeding inside. I couldn't hurt as much as I did, without there being some horrible wound deep inside me.

"When the kids woke up, I gave them breakfast and then told Jonathan that you had spent the night on the boat. He only shrugged, as if to say, 'Who cares?'

"After breakfast I knew I had to go and speak with you. I wanted the confrontation to take place away from home, so the kids wouldn't hear us, because I knew it would be the mother of all confrontations."

Robert nodded. "Yes, it was." He didn't smile.

"And I also knew it would be the last confrontation we would ever have in our marriage. I couldn't go through another scenario like this. Ever again."

"I understand you were suffering." Robert reached out to put a hand on her shoulder, but Marshall moved as far away as possible in the confines of the car.

Her eyes filled and then overflowed. She wiped her cheeks with the back of her hand and gulped. "Don't touch me."

She drives back to the marina. Fury gives her the determination to march to where the boat is docked. As she gets on board, the rocking alerts him to her presence and soon his head appears from below. He glares at her with repulsive, unfocused eyes that are filled with anger.

"Wha' ya doin' here?" His voice slurs. "Do ya even realize wha' you did? Do ya know how difficult it was to stop this fuckin' thing from hittin' our neighbours' boats? Don' ya have any respect for our neighbours?"

She ignores his ranting and looks into the cabin. There sits a man, beer bottle in hand, every bit as bleary-eyed as Robert.

"Get out of here!" she says to him, her voice loud and firm. "Right this instant."

"Ya go' no right orderin' my frien' aroun'!" Robert yells at her. He turns to the man and stammers, "Don' ya listen to my fuckin' wife. Ya stay right there."

But the fellow, obviously frightened by her stormy face, quickly slinks off as she turns to face Robert. This is the absolute end.

The silence inside the car was palpable.

Had Robert been able to absorb all she'd told him? Marshall still sat, crouched as far away as possible from him. She couldn't stop trembling.

"Do you see now?" she breathed. "Can you imagine how I felt when I knew for a fact that you were dead?"

"I . . . yes, I'm trying to imagine. It must have been horrible."

"You don't get it, do you?" She wasn't angry, only resigned. "You don't understand how it feels when you know someone you love is dead. And I *knew* you were dead. You simply couldn't have done such a horrible, hurtful thing if you'd been alive."

"I understand."

But did he? She saw he wanted to, but no one could, except someone who had gone through it.

As the minutes passed, her breathing became calmer. She was thankful he didn't try to take her in his arms. She needed room to compose herself without his interference.

"I was drained of energy," she continued after a while. "I couldn't eat for a week. Nothing mattered but getting away from you, before you could hurt me again." She turned to look out, not wanting to see his face. He was trying too hard to look chagrinned. "I never will understand how a man could do what you did to me . . . to the woman you professed to love."

"Marshall, please believe me, I do love you. Now even more than in those carefree days when I took everything for granted—even your love. But I definitely can understand why you had to get away from me."

He reached a hand out but didn't touch her. "I know I have an awful lot of making up to do and I don't blame you if you'll never be able to forgive me. But, dammit, I'm going to try!"

Marshall looked at him now, because his voice sounded authentic, like he really meant it.

"Seeing you again made me realize there's no choice for me but to try to win you back," Robert went on. "Without you, life has no meaning. I love you and I want to live with you again. And if the only way that can happen is through dating, then let's start dating. The sooner we get the show on the road, the sooner you'll be mine again."

She sprang around to face him, almost making him jump back in his seat. "This is not about sex, Robert!"

"Of course not," he sputtered."That's not what I meant."

Sure he didn't! She knew that was exactly what he meant.

For some time he sat, looking sulky, like he'd always done when he knew he was in the wrong and didn't want to admit it.

"Listen," he said at last. "I'm really trying to stop thinking like that, but it's not easy, because I've missed you and I want you so desperately."

When she shifted away again, he put up a hand. "Don't worry. I promise I'll behave the way you want."

If only he knew how much she didn't want him to

"behave". How much she wanted to stop all this, and just have him take her in his arms and close this gap between them.

But she was scared. Deadly afraid this could all end up a horrible train wreck.

But then she saw a flash of fear in his eyes and realized she wasn't the only one who had these awful doubts.

"Do you know what I do when I think I'll mess up?" Robert said, unexpectedly opening up. "When I get those awful self-doubts I think about that little book I used to read to Jonathan when he was a toddler. 'I think I can! I think I can!' Remember it?"

She nodded. "Yes."

"That's been my mantra throughout those endless days of self-imposed sobriety. And when I conquer another day, I tell myself, 'I knew I could, I knew I could'!" He grinned sheepishly and stole an embarrassed glance at her.

Marshall's heart went out to him, but she let him go on without touching him.

"For the past nine years I've been saying that to myself every night after another day of victory. But—" he swallowed. "I'm sure you realize I can't ever be sure that one day I won't—"

"All right, then," she broke in before he said those frightening words. "Let's give it a try."

His face brightened up like the ray of sunshine. He let out his breath in a sigh of relief and smiled broadly. "Then for our first date, I'd like to ask you out for dinner. Is tonight too soon?"

"Yes, it is. I first have to explain things to Steve."

The joy in his eyes was replaced by anger. "What things?" he asked grudgingly. "You don't owe him anything."

"I do. He asked me to marry him," Marshall said quietly but firmly.

Robert's Adam's apple moved as he swallowed hard. "And have you . . .?"

Marshall knew he was trying hard to keep his jealousy in check. "I haven't said yes."

Triumph made him sound smug. "Why not?"

"I wasn't sure how Olivia would take to having him in the house. I was waiting till she went to college next year."

He looked stunned. "You were going to marry him in a year? So if I had waited just a bit longer, it would have been too late?"

"Yes, probably."

"Do you love him?" His voice was harsh and demanding.

"No."

His quick laugh expressed his relief. "Then why would you marry him?"

"He's good for me. He's reliable and dependable and steady and—"

"Those are all the same thing," Robert pointed out tersely. "What else?"

"He gives me comfort and security. He's a nice man."

"Nice? Like how?"

"Robert, Steve's and my relationship has nothing to do with you and I refuse to feed your jealousy by telling you about him."

Robert gave a short, cynical laugh. "Feed my jealousy? Who's jealous?"

"You are. So we won't discuss this issue any longer. I'll tell Steve that you've appeared out of the blue and we're going to see if we can make anything out of the tatters of our old relationship."

"Hey, don't make it sound so positive, will you?" Robert interjected gloomily. "Or this Steve will keep lurking around, just waiting for our old tattered relationship to fall apart."

But Marshall didn't offer him any comfort. "He might," she stated simply. "He loves me, and he just might decide to wait around and see what transpires. As you just said, nothing is certain between you and me."

"Except that I love you." Now Robert reached out and firmly pulled her to him. "And you love me," he murmured against her hair.

Marshall was too exhausted to resist, and leaned her head against his shoulder. "Yes. I know," she said with a sigh. "Even though I said I didn't, I have never stopped loving you."

But as Robert hold tightened, she placed her hands between them, palms against his chest. "Please understand that for me it's important to have a peaceful and contented life." She said the next words firmly, clearly, so there would be no misunderstanding. "Even if that means living without you."

"Peaceful and contented?" Robert burst out. "No, I can't understand that! You're sounding like an octogenarian, for chrissake. Our relationship used to be fun and lively. Deliriously happy, even. Surely you want that back again. Surely peaceful and contented can't ever compete with happy and fun."

"Living a peaceful life makes me happy. I don't need fun."

Robert held her by the shoulders and stared at her

incredulously. "Marshall! You're only forty-nine years old, not eighty-nine! You can be peaceful in your grave."

"Don't be facetious, Robert. You know what I mean." Marshall sat up and buckled on her seatbelt, showing him she was ready to go. "Now, please drive me back to school for my car. I'll call you after I've spoken to Steve and we're free to start this . . . this dating business."

"This dating business?" Robert grumbled. "Boy, you really make it sound exciting." He pressed the start button and brought the engine to life.

"Robert, don't you see I'm frightened? I'm scared to death I'm getting into something I'll regret for the rest of my days." What if he fell off the wagon? They would lose each other forever, because there was no way on earth she would ever get on that merry-go-round again.

Robert put the car in reverse and looked over his shoulder as he backed out onto the road. He turned to face her before driving on. "Marshall, I know damn well I'll only have one kick at the can."

Yes, she knew he was as frightened as she.

Quiet music played in the background. Their table was in a discreet, secluded corner of the restaurant, with large plants giving protection from any eyes that might pry into their privacy. On the table a candle flickered with a romantic glow.

"Seduction is written all over this scene," Marshall remarked, although she knew very well that her outfit also mirrored that very same thing. The wine-red dress with spaghetti straps hugged her figure alluringly. It was done on purpose, of course, for she wasn't above trying to make Robert drool. Since she was now considerably older than the last time they'd been out like this, she wanted to prove to herself that she was still desirable. "But it's not going to work, my dear."

Robert sighed but didn't look annoyed. "Oh, for chrissake, could you try to be a bit more romantic? You know how much trouble I had getting this very table? Although, I would much rather have taken you to my hotel room and—"

"So, why did you want this very table?" Marshall broke in. Of course she knew. This had been their favorite restaurant for romantic occasions, birthdays and anniversaries, and this had been their special, secluded table. But her pretend-amnesia didn't work.

"You're not fooling me, you beautiful doll," Robert retorted, squeezing her hand across the table. "You know why I chose this place for tonight. In fact if I hadn't, I would've heard about it." His voice changed to that of an annoyed woman. "You say you love me and you didn't even remember our special restaurant."

Marshall laughed. He was right, of course. Somehow it felt so comfortable to be with someone who could read her like a book and didn't try to be polite and overly-correct around her.

Like Steve. It was as though the man was always being so careful not to disrupt her calm. Sometimes it got uncomfortably stifling, and she felt like shouting, "Oh for Pete's sake, Steve! Let down your guard and say something stupid for a change!" But it wasn't his fault if he'd been brought up to be so very considerate, almost to the point of annoyance.

She felt a twinge of sorrow thinking how sad Steve had looked when she'd told him that Robert had returned and they were going to give their relationship a try.

"But you've always said how happy you're with me," Steve had insisted. "And how awful life was with him."

He wouldn't understand, of course, and it was no use trying to explain. "That's true. I am happy. And yes, it was awful. Toward the end it was hell, and with you life has been peaceful. But I've never stopped loving him, Steve. If I had, I would've married you by now."

Steve was wounded, she knew that, but there was nothing she could do to make him feel any better. He was such a good man that he deserved someone who loved him for himself, and not just as a calm, secure harbour.

"I'll wait for you," he'd said with so much hope in his voice that it almost made her cry. "In case things don't work out, I'll be here."

"No!" she cried. "Steve, I don't want you to wait for me! You have a life to live."

"Not without you, I don't."

"Steve, please . . ." She reached out her hands to him, appealing for his understanding.

He took them and as he held them in both of his, Marshall felt the security that his touch had always produced. She remembered the first time he'd put his arm around her when they had been sitting side by side on the couch. She'd leaned her head on his shoulder and for the first time in years she'd felt comfort and peace flow through her.

"And if you need a shoulder to cry on while this experiment is going on, please call me."

That did it. The tears came and she did just what he'd asked. She pressed her face against his shoulder and sobbed while he held her against his breast.

At last she raised her head and delivered the final blow. "Steve, even if this experiment doesn't pan out, I will not be returning to you." She felt like a murderer.

"I love you, Marshall. I always will." Steve said it so tenderly that a fresh burst of tears sent her head onto his shoulder again.

But no way was she going to let him stand in the wings waiting for his turn. She made her voice as decisive as she could, without sounding brutal. "I simply cannot have you sit there, waiting for my train to crash. You're such a good man that I want you to look for someone who is deserving of your devotion. Do you understand me?"

"I do. And if that's what you want, I promise I will." But his inconsolably sad face told her he wasn't going to try very hard.

Marshall freed herself from his embrace, dug out a tissue and blew her nose. "Good," she said decidedly.

That was another thing that had bothered her about him. Steve had always done what she'd asked, without question, like an obedient puppy. Even now, when he'd been given the brush-off.

Robert, on the other hand, would argue to make his point, until it became obvious he was wrong. And he would tease her mercilessly at times, and even make her furious, but he could always make her laugh. She'd forgotten how seldom she really laughed nowadays.

The background music in the restaurant was discreet, but suddenly Marshall became aware of the selection that was playing. It was an orchestral version of "You are My Destiny," and her heart sang along. No matter what, she had to admit, Robert was her destiny. It was as simple as that.

And as complicated as that.

"You're not wearing any rings," Robert now observed, still holding her hand. "Where are the ones I gave you, if you don't mind me asking?"

She lowered her eyes and withdrew her hand. "Yes, I do mind you asking." No way was she going to admit they were safely tucked in her jewelry box, along with her grandmother's silver cross pendant and other precious mementos from the past. "Because it's none of your business. But if you really want to know, I have no idea where they are."

But she didn't fool him.

"You have them stowed away somewhere safe. Right?"

"I told you I don't know where they are. Exactly."

Robert burst out laughing. His laughter was deep and sexy as ever, and Marshall realized how much she'd missed hearing it.

"My darling Marsha, you're incredible! Of course you don't know *exactly* where they are, right down to the precise millimeter. But I'm pretty sure you know their approximate location in your house. Correct?"

She never had learned the art of telling little white lies, and he knew it. "Yes, they're somewhere," she conceded. "Maybe in the garbage? And do not call me Marsha!" she said with a threatening frown.

The waiter came up just as Robert's laughter rang out jubilantly. The man smiled broadly at the happy couple and handed the wine list to Robert.

"Can I bring you something to drink?"

Marshall froze. She couldn't look at Robert, who scanned the wine list as though he were actually planning to order something from it. Cold fear plucked at her nerves at the mere thought.

Robert closed the list and handed it back to the waiter. "A glass of merlot for the lady, and I'll have a large ginger ale. No ice."

Marshall heaved a sigh of relief. "You didn't have to order wine for me," she protested after the waiter had left. "I don't want to—" How did one say "tempt you" without sounding like she didn't trust him around alcohol?

Robert reached for her hand again and clasped it warmly. "Marshall, since we're going to be going on these dates for—not too long, I hope—I want you to know that it's perfectly okay for you to indulge in your favorite glass of wine, even with me sitting in front of you. It's my problem, not yours. And I promise not to drool on the table."

Now it was she who burst out laughing, melting the tension. And when the drinks arrived, she was able to enjoy hers with only a tiny sliver of guilt.

Marshall saw his Adam's apple move in the way that told her he wasn't totally comfortable with the scene.

"What's the matter?" she asked and laid her hand softly on his clenched fist. At her touch his fingers uncurled and he relaxed visibly.

He grinned. "Just some old ghosts from the past trying to intrude on our first date."

"Let's not allow them. Here's to us." In the olden days they'd always entwined their arms to take a sip from each other's glass, and out of habit she reached over to do the gesture.

Simultaneously they both pulled back.

"Abort, abort," Robert joked, while Marshall lowered her gaze to avoid his eyes.

"It's all right," Robert said quietly and touched her hair. "We'll get used to it. I think of it as someone saying to a blind person, 'See you tomorrow'. It's just the way people talk, and the ones who can't see or can't drink, they just carry on naturally. They're not offended. In fact, when there's alcohol around, I feel better if people just act normal, without twisting themselves into pretzels trying not to offend me."

Marshall tried to smile, though her insides were still shaking from the close call. "I'll get used to it, I promise. It's just that I'm not on my guard yet about these things."

Robert's sudden anger hit her on the face. "That's just the point!" His voice rose a notch. "Look at you, sitting there squirming. I don't want you to be on your guard. I don't want you to watch what you say. I want you to say things just the way you've always said them. I want you to behave the way you've always behaved. And I want you to say the word 'alcohol' without stuttering."

"I'm sorry." Still she couldn't look at him in the eyes.

Robert heaved an impatient sigh. "Stop being sorry. Say it now. Say 'alcohol'."

Marshall coughed to clear her throat. "Alcohol." It came out weak and fuzzy, and she knew he wasn't happy with her effort.

"Again," he commanded. "Say 'alcoholic'".

Marshall felt the heat rise to her cheeks. "Now you're being silly."

His brow furrowed. "Say it!"

"Alcoholic," she spat out. "There, now are you happy?"

"No, but I want you to promise you'll repeat it at home ten times every night, till the next time we meet. Then we won't have to go through this nonsense again, I hope."

"I'll feel silly, but I promise to do my homework."

Once again he took her hands into his. "All I can do is hold your hand, while my mind keeps telling me to take you in my arms and crush you against me," he complained. His fingers tightened their hold. "Marshall, you are so desirable tonight I'm ready to carry you off behind that big, potted palm and—"

A discreet cough stopped him from executing his plan. The waiter had appeared silently and now stood beside them ready to take their order.

Robert gave a short laugh. "Sorry, we haven't had a chance to look at the menu yet. A couple more minutes?"

As they waited for their food, Marshall laid into him. "And if I have to do homework, you do, too!" she fumed. "I don't want to be embarrassed by these juvenile statements in public. Repeat ten times every night, 'I will not say embarrassing things in public'."

"Okay. But in private I'm allowed to say whatever embarrassing things come to mind, right? I want to be able to worship you with words, if not with my body. The latter is, by the way, what the minister ordered me to do when we got married, remember? And I'd much rather do that than just talk about it."

"Well, we're not married now," Marshall said as sternly as she could. But just thinking about what he was capable of doing caused her heart to skip a few beats. "So, your hands you'll keep to yourself. Remember that."

"You are a cruel woman, but I did promise, didn't I?"

"Yes, you did." She made sure her voice didn't reflect the trembling and yearning his words had created inside her.

"This Friday night I want to take you to a movie," Robert proposed. "Like we used to do when we first started dating way back in high school."

"I'll be too tired from teaching all week," Marshall protested. Things were moving fast. Maybe too fast? "My class this year has been a handful. Lovely, bright kids, but boy, are they active."

"What better way to relax than in my affable company? First we'll grab a bite to eat at some greasy spoon, just the way we used to do, and then we'll catch the last show. Agreed?"

Marshall knew it was no use trying to kid herself. Or him. This was what she wanted to do, just as much as he did.

He reached for her hand, which Marshall surrendered to him willingly. It was no use trying to pretend that she didn't want him to touch her. She did. Her whole body was begging her to loosen up and allow him to take her to his hotel room as he had suggested earlier. They belonged in bed together, not here, with electric currents coursing from his fingers into hers.

Was she being a total idiot denying herself the sweetness, the thrill, of making love with him? She knew exactly what it would be like to have sex with Robert. That had always been the single aspect of their relationship that had united them while his drinking had torn them apart.

No! She was doing the right thing. The unpleasant thing would be to keep reminding herself of the painful past in order to shore up her resolve. But there was no other way. She would have to build a strong barricade to protect herself from his charms and from the desire that roiled inside her own wanton body.

The question was—could she do it?

Chapter Five

Robert sat at the hotel sports bar, staring at one of the several TVs. Straight ahead, he could watch hockey players fighting, gloves dropped, sticks flung across the ice. Turning his head left, he could watch two bloodied guys kick-boxing. To his right was a much more civilized game of football with big muddied guys piling up on one of their fellow players.

He tried to hold on to the picture of the woman who had sat across the table from him tonight at dinner. His heart swelled with love. She'd been so beautiful, with her bare, smooth shoulders glowing in the candlelight. Her reddish blond hair, usually in loose curls around her oval face, had been held up by glittering combs, giving her that sophisticated, sexy look he loved.

Obviously she'd taken care to look as alluring as possible and it stoked his ego to think she had purposely tried to seduce him—and had succeeded brilliantly. If only he could have had his way, they would have walked out of the restaurant and driven straight to his hotel room. Forget the dinner! But he knew it would have been worse than useless to even propose that. And not only useless, but probably lethal, jeopardizing his whole plan.

Lucky for him, he wasn't operating in the dark. Not like some fellow in a brand new relationship, just starting out, wondering which actions would please his woman and which would annoy her. He could read Marshall like a book, based on twelve years of living together and seven years of intense dating before that. Of course she could have changed, but he doubted her likes and dislikes would have altered too much. And surely her basic personality would have remained the same, despite the ups and downs of the intervening years.

He thought of how her blue eyes had sparkled when she'd laughed, and the sound still lingered in his ears. If only he could always keep her that happy. If only he were certain he could keep away from . . . No! He forced down the self-doubts and fears that had tried to push themselves into their first evening together.

He hoped this operation could be speeded up, because living in a hotel, the evenings were the worst, with nothing constructive to pass his time. He wanted to be with Marshall every night, but he knew she wanted to concentrate on her school lessons during week nights.

What had he done at home during the evenings when they were married and she did her school work? He cringed. The last few years he would've been slouching in front of the TV with a glass of vodka, more than likely flaking out before the evening was over. If he was home at all. During the weekends, he would've been sailing with his buddies or out drinking, being dropped off at his doorstep by a taxi at some late hour.

Robert held his head in his hands, trying to squeeze out the memories. If he hadn't been drunk most of the time, what could he have been doing instead? He could have been reading the newspaper or a book. Or puttering around in his workshop. Or playing with his baby daughter. Or going to watch his son's baseball games, playing catch with him in the back yard, helping him with his homework, or reading aloud to him, like a good father.

God! All the things he could have, and should have been doing. And instead he'd ruined everyone's life with his drinking.

The bartender stopped in front of him."What can I get you?"

"Vodka," Robert answered automatically. Damn! Too late he realized what he'd done. It would look strange for him to call out to the bartender and cancel his order.

The glass sat in front of him and he smelled the familiar fumes, remembering how smoothly the liquid had gone down. It had created a welcome state of numbness that stopped him from thinking about the past. About Marshall. About Jonathan. And about the baby. The baby, who no longer was a baby but a teenager—almost a young woman, whom he didn't know at all. He hoped his drinking hadn't hurt her. Hoped she'd been too young to understand about the pain he'd caused her mother and brother.

Robert gripped the glass as his heart was squeezed by a pair of vice grips. What he'd done to his family was unforgiveable.

God! He really, really needed this drink. He knew it would help erase—at least for a while—this painful feeling of guilt inside him. And even temporary relief was better than putting up with this ache in his gut. He brought the vodka up to his nose and breathed in deeply, hungrily.

No! He slammed the glass down and droplets of liquid spilled onto the counter. What right did he have to try to escape the pain? He didn't deserve forgetfulness. Because of him, Marshall and Jonathan had suffered, and they had no way to numb the pain other than bury it deep inside them.

Bury it! That's exactly what Marshall had done. He hoped that action had somehow helped her to deal with it. But how was Jonathan handling his own buried pain? Robert had to be big enough to accept and understand it, and try to work through it.

He dug some bills out of his pocket and placed them on the counter. A brisk walk in the bracing spring night would do him more good than sitting at the bar, tempting himself.

Despite everything, he could once again pat himself on the back for another day of sobriety.

"So have you revealed to our children the fact that their parents are dating?" Robert asked. He and Marshall sat in a booth at Humphrey's Diner where hamburgers and fries replaced the gourmet meal of their first date.

Marshall picked up a fry and chewed it thoroughly before replying. That was precisely the one thing she hadn't yet come to grips with in this new development. She'd spoken to Steve, but not to Olivia and Jonathan, because she wasn't sure how they would react. And she wasn't prepared to risk a negative outcome. Besides, she rationalized, it wasn't just her job to do the revealing. Robert was as much a part of this conundrum as she was.

"You know, Robert . . ." Marshall began and wiped her mouth to gain more time.

Robert's fingers drummed on the tabletop as he waited for her response, while she tried to suppress her smile. Obviously he was still as impatient as ever. It was so easy to get him to sweat, and she knew just which buttons to press. Of course he could do the same to her. Perversely, the thought made her feel warm inside because it was comfortable to be with someone who knew her so well. Yes, even if he sometimes used this knowledge to tease and annoy her on purpose.

"Yes?" he now asked. "What's on your mind? Spit it out."

"I don't think it's just my job to tell the children about us. I think we should do it together. I was thinking maybe I would invite Jonathan for dinner on Sunday, if he's available, and you'll come over and then we'll talk. How does that sound?"

"Besides scary?"

"I don't know why it should scare you. They're your kids."

Robert raised an eyebrow. "Sure, that's what women always tell their husbands."

Marshall almost choked on the fry she had just put into her mouth. "That's a fine thing to say!" It was impossible to keep her laughter from bubbling out.

Robert bit into his burger. "Okay, of course I know they're my kids," he said with his mouth full. "But I don't *know* them at all. Even Jonathan, whom I should know—I don't." He sobered. "I'm afraid when he was small, those weren't my model-father years."

Marshall saw regret and shame flash on his face,

but she didn't try to comfort him. For this he didn't deserve any pity. "No, they weren't. And that's something you'll have to come to grips with on your own."

He looked dejected. "I know."

"And you have to realize you're not dating a single woman, but a mother. A fiercely protective, dedicated mother."

Robert looked down and pushed the fries around on his plate with his fork. "I do realize that. Although—and I hate to admit this—I wasn't thinking of the kids when I saw you and sent you the flowers. It was you I wanted back, not Olivia and Jonathan." He raised his eyes and beamed them into hers, and in their depths Marshall could read this non-model-father's shame, sadness and regret.

"And frankly," he muttered, "the thought of meeting them scares the hell out of me."

Marshal refused to take his hand, although she was filled with empathy for him. "I know it's scary, but it has to be done. So how about we both bite the bullet and get it over with this Sunday? I'll call you if Jonathan isn't available, but in any case can you come for dinner at six?"

He nodded, his mouth in a grim, hard line. "Yeah, I'll be there."

He took her hand and they sat in silence until Robert spoke. His voice was thick with emotion. "You know, Marshall, holding your hand is almost as good as being in bed with you. In some way it's even better, because now it's just pure love I feel flowing between us, without the sex."

Marshall smiled. "In that case, perhaps we ought to always just hold hands and not bring sex into the picture to spoil it?" That should tease him out of his melancholy.

He took the bait. "No sex?" he yelped, causing three heads to turn in the booth across the aisle.

"Shh!" Marshall cautioned him. "Remember what I said about blurting out embarrassing things in public?"

"Sorry, but your statement was so outrageous I couldn't help myself. Maybe you shouldn't say things in public you know will upset me and cause me to say embarrassing things in public."

Marshall laughed. "Enough of this nonsense!" She picked up her purse. "Let's get to the movie before the show is over."

They walked over to the nearby theatre and sneaked inside in the middle of the show. In the dark they found seats near the back. But the intimacy created by the darkness made it impossible for Robert to concentrate on anything but the woman beside him. Although the fast-paced spy flick was trying its best to get his attention, he hardly gave it a glance. He was totally absorbed in Marshall, snug in the crook of his arm. How many movies had gone unwatched in their early days of dating?

He nuzzled his cheek against her soft hair. He could swear it smelled of the same, familiar shampoo, and overwhelming tenderness filled him. How he loved this woman! How could he have lived all these years without her?

"You're still using 'Honey Blossom' shampoo," he whispered.

Surprised, Marshall turned her face up to him. Her lips came to within a hair's breadth of his. "You remember?" she whispered.

Briefly he brushed his lips against hers and sighed with longing. "Uh-huh. They say the sense of smell is the last to go."

"I always thought it was hearing."

"No, I think hearing's the first. But neither of mine is gone yet. And I have other senses that are pretty acute, too. Like lust!" He breathed the last word right into her ear.

Marshall clamped her palm against his mouth. "Shh. And that's not a sense. That's a—"

"Whatever it is, it's on the rise." The action on the screen thundered at excessively high decibel, so he spoke low, rather than whispering.

Just then the tumult ceased.

"Shh." The woman in front of them turned to glare at them.

Like a pair of guilty kids they slid down in their seats, shoulders shaking with laughter. Robert's arm remained around her shoulders and now it tightened, pulling her as close to him as possible.

"What are we doing here?" he whispered. "We should go to my hotel room."

"That's precisely where we are not going," Marshall whispered back. "Aren't you enjoying the movie?"

"What movie?" Robert knew she hadn't been watching it, either. He began to nibble her earlobe and imagined picking her up in his arms and carrying her away.

"You chose it. I thought you wanted to see it," she whispered.

The woman turned her head again. "Shh."

Robert her and nuzzled Marshall's cheek. "Chose what?"

"Shh."

Marshall sat up and moved away from him.

"Let's go," she whispered. "We're being nuisances."

As they rose, she gave an apologetic smile to the scowling woman who craned her neck to make sure they left.

Once outside in the dark spring evening, they stood undecided in front of the theatre under the marquee lights.

"It was getting downright embarrassing in there," Marshall said, severely.

Robert ignored her school-teacher voice. "It's a balmy evening for this time of year. Let's walk for a while."

"And hold hands?"

"Definitely." He brought her hand up and kissed the palm. "Mmm. Nice."

"I said hold hands, not kiss them."

"Your cruelty is beyond belief."

Marshall's insides were quivering with nervous tension. Dinner was in the oven and guileless Olivia, oblivious to her mother's angst, was circling around the kitchen, nibbling on a cherry tomato she'd swiped from the salad.

"What gives, Mom? What's with all these goodies?" The girl reached for a piece of cheese from a tray and then ducked her mother's swinging tea towel. "I'm getting hungry," she grumbled. "If Steve's not on time, he'll have to eat the leftovers."

"Steve's not coming tonight." Marshall tried to keep her voice nonchalant and turned to rearrange the cheese tray so Olivia wouldn't see her face.

"He's not?" Olivia grabbed a cracker before she fled into the family room. "He always comes for Sunday dinners," she called from there.

"Not always," Marshall corrected her. "The operative word is 'often'."

Olivia slumped onto the couch beside Jonathan. "In my books often is the same as always, Mrs. Teacher. So who's coming? Surely all this isn't just for old Jonathan here." She poked her brother in the ribs with her finger. "He doesn't deserve fancy food. He doesn't visit us often enough. Too busy with his work to bother with his family."

Marshall came and laid the tray of cheese and crackers on the coffee table. "Chartered accountants are busy people, especially at tax time."

Jonathan glanced at her before speaking. "It's Dad." He looked through his beer glass at the light fixture in the ceiling. "Isn't it? That's why you were so keen for me to come."

Olivia jumped up. "Daddy's coming?" she squealed. "Is that right, Mom?"

Marshall could only nod. Her voice had completely left her.

"Why didn't you tell me?" Olivia yelled. "I'm a mess! I thought it was just Steve."

She leapt up the stairs two at a time and a moment later the walls shook as her bedroom door slammed.

"Yeah, why didn't you tell us?" Jonathan's voice was accusing. "I thought it was just Steve, too. But I figured maybe you two were going to announce your engagement, or something. Your dinner invitation sounded so formal, and you sounded so nervous."

Damn the boy's intuitive ears! Marshall didn't think she'd sounded *that* nervous. But maybe she had, considering she'd been apprehensive and agitated all week.

"First of all," she began, and knew she sounded defensive. "I don't appreciate both of you saying 'just Steve', as though the man was an insignificant nobody. He's a very kind, generous man and he's been good to us all."

"I'm sorry. Of course he is," Jonathan mumbled. "I didn't mean to make it sound like that."

Now that she'd gained the upper hand, Marshall went on with more confidence. "I didn't tell you about your father because I know how you feel about him and I was afraid you wouldn't come. And as for Olivia, I wanted to surprise her. Thanks for spoiling that," she added, striving to gain some more advantage by sounding accusing. A small battle was shaping up here, she realized, but she was too unsure of herself to give quarter.

"And how, exactly, do I feel about him?" Jonathan's eyebrows rose in a sardonic arc. "Maybe you could enlighten me because I sure as hell don't have any idea how I—"

The doorbell rang and both mother and son started. But then Jonathan sat back and took a gulp of beer, putting on an air of nonchalance.

Marshall smoothed down her skirt as she hurried to the door.

Robert stood on the steps and greeted her with a wide grin and a bouquet of spring flowers. "Hi, gorgeous!"

She sent a sidelong warning frown in the direction of the family room.

Robert's smile faded and without ceremony he thrust the tulips and daffodils into her hands.

"Come in, Robert," Marshall said in an overly bright voice, loud enough for anyone in the neighborhood to hear.

She clutched the bouquet to her breast like a shield as they entered the family room. To her relief, Jonathan got up, albeit with deliberate slowness and a total lack of enthusiasm. If he had remained slouched on the couch Marshall would have killed him on the spot.

But he made no move to approach his father.

Marshall desperately willed her heart to stop thumping, afraid the men would see the bouquet shaking against her breast. She opened her mouth to say some carefully rehearsed words, but they were stuck somewhere deep down in her throat.

They all stood looking at one another other until Marshall finally managed to croak, "Jonathan, you remember your father?"

She knew her phony, bright smile wasn't fooling anyone. "Robert, as you can see, your son has become a fine young man." Such stupid words. Was that really what she'd practiced over and over in the sleepless hours last night? Surely not.

"Yes. How are you?" Although Robert's voice did have a slight conciliatory tone, the words were pronounced stiffly. Neither man made a move to reach out to shake hands with the other. The word "son" was left hanging in the air between them and almost made Marshall cry out in pain.

"Fine."

This was not going well. But of course she hadn't expected the two would slap each other on the back and start a chummy conversation about baseball the minute they set eyes on each other. She had to give them time.

Lots of time.

"So, shall we sit down while we wait for Olivia?" Marshall said, the phony smile still pasted on her face. She wanted to run out the door and scream in pain. She needed to get away so she could double over and clutch her stomach to stop the horrible ache inside her. But she remained standing, praying Olivia would come down and let her escape into the kitchen.

Jonathan flopped back on the couch, taking up as much room as possible. Robert sat on the love seat, opposite him.

"Where did that girl disappear to, anyway?" Marshall fretted. She hastily picked up the cheese tray, offered it to the two men, but both refused. She set the tray back on the table and sat down on the edge of the ottoman.

"She heard he was coming so she went to change," Jonathan said with a shrug that obviously wasn't meant to be subtle.

Marshall's heart convulsed. He was coming. He. Not Dad. Jonathan was dismissing his father right in his face. Impolite boy. No, not even a boy any more. How could her own son be so rude?

"We thought Steve was coming tonight." Now Jonathan looked at his father but his words were obviously meat to hurt, not inform. At that moment Marshall realized that Jonathan, no longer a boy, knew how to use jealousy as a tool and stick it to his father. "He often comes for Sunday dinner. Steve's a really great guy."

"Not any more, he won't be coming," Marshall snapped. She wanted Jonathan to shut up before Robert's face could turn any stormier.

Jonathan reached for his beer with studied purposefulness and, first giving his lips a lick, he took a long swig. The satisfied "Ahh!" that followed was like a blaring taunt to his father and Marshall saw Robert's eyes narrow with anger.

But just then, to Marshall's great relief, she heard Olivia skipping down the stairs. That made them all turn, and brought the appalling performance to a halt.

"Sorry I'm late!" the girl caroled even before she flitted into the room.

Marshall knew very well that Olivia's bright voice hid her nervousness. She was a great actress. Like her mother.

At the entrance to the family room the girl came to a dramatic stop. "Oh, hi!"

Her surprised expression at seeing Robert was also not the genuine article, but worked well under the circumstances. She struck a pose that was obviously meant to charm. It was easy to tell she'd chosen her outfit with the specific purpose of showing her new father what a cute daughter he had.

Robert rose slowly to greet her, but Marshall bounced right up, full of nervous energy.

"Darling, this is your father. I know you don't remember him, but you've seen pictures of him. Hasn't your daughter grown, Robert?" Why was she saying these stupid things? Blah, blah, blah.

"And into a most charming young lady," Robert said as Olivia came toward him with a huge smile of genuine pleasure. She didn't exactly jump into his arms, but she did plant a small kiss on his cheek.

Marshall exhaled at long last and the pain inside her subsided ever so slightly.

"Hi, Daddy," Olivia said with simple sincerity that made Robert smile broadly.

"Hello, Olivia," he said in his deep, smooth-as-velvet

voice and gave his daughter a hug.

Not a bear hug, but a quick hug that made Marshall weak with relief. It sufficed for the moment. Mission accomplished. Or at least half a mission. She glared at Jonathan who pretended not to bother watching the proceedings. The moment was almost spoiled for her, but not quite. One out of two wasn't bad for round one.

Robert sat down and Olivia snuggled right next to her new-found, handsome father. It was easy to see she was already infatuated with him and kept up a lively chatter about her school, her friends, and with whatever came into her head. And Marshall was infinitely grateful for every syllable the girl uttered.

If Jonathan or Marshall had prattled on in that fashion it would have been a sign of absolute terror. But for Olivia this twittering was normal, and didn't indicate nervousness on her part. It was just Olivia. Her volubility allowed Marshall to go into the kitchen and look after the dinner preparations without worrying about leaving Robert in the room alone with Jonathan and his sullen silence.

She could hear Robert respond with appropriate noises, and ask relevant questions that kept Olivia talking. Marshall knew he was using his daughter as a shield to prevent having to deal with his son's attitude.

Chapter Six

Marshall stared with sleepless eyes into the darkness. She had to face twenty-three seven-year-olds in the morning and the second consecutive night of lying awake didn't bode well for the coming day. But she couldn't stop rehashing everything that had happened.

The dinner and the rest of the evening had passed in a blur of nervous energy. She had definitely operated on adrenalin alone. Only Olivia had saved her from collapsing into a sobbing heap on the kitchen floor between courses.

Jonathan and Robert had been like two bulls, just short of glowering at each other, and it had taken all her willpower to keep from running out, screeching in frustration. Marshall knew that Jonathan's good upbringing—no thanks to Robert—was the only thing that had kept him civil. Just barely so. Nary a word had passed between them, and Marshall could hardly blame Robert for not trying harder to make overtures toward his son. The young man had been about as open and approachable as a locked safe.

She turned onto her side and sighed. Come on, sleep.

The revelation that their parents were dating—and that Steve was now out of the picture forever—was greeted with great glee by Olivia, and with a disdainful shrug by Jonathan.

"Whatever," had been his comment and Marshall had felt like boxing his ears for his attitude. If she'd announced that they were going to have pizza for dinner the next day his reaction might have been more enthusiastic.

Time. Time. She had to give him time. Give them both time.

After Robert left, Marshall had turned to Jonathan pouring out all the hurt of the evening on him.

"Couldn't you have been just a teensy bit more flexible? Just a tad more friendly?" she hurled at him. "You were like the proverbial Sphinx, for Pete's sake!"

Her rebuke had been met by angry, narrowed eyes. So like his father's, she remembered with a shudder.

"What did you want me to do?" he demanded. "Bring out my football and gush, 'Hey, Pop! Wanna go out an' toss some pigskin with me, huh, Pop?' Would that have made you happy?"

"No, it would not have. Unless you meant it."

"Meant it?" Jonathan snorted. "I wouldn't have even dreamed of doing it!"

But Marshall knew that many times as a child he'd dreamed of doing just that, wishing that his dad would give him even a fraction of the attention he gave to his vodka bottle. She knew. And even now it wrenched her heart to remember how Jonathan had tried so hard to please,wanting so much to be Daddy's boy.

"Hey, Daddy, c'n I hold the tiller? I know how to steer

the boat."

"You won't know what to do if things get rough."

"Yeah, but it's not too windy now. C'n I please? Mr. Sherwin always lets his kids steer their C&C."

"All right, but hold it steady."

Marshall can see how reluctant Robert is to turn over this job. Sitting at the helm, lazily holding a beer can is his picture of the ideal sailor. She breathes a sigh of relief when he consents to relinquish the task to his son. It means so much to Jonathan.

Eagerly the boy grabs the tiller and immediately the wind goes out of the sails.

"Oops! Sorry. I think I turned it a bit too much."

"Who told you to turn it?" Robert growls and Marshall sees Jonathan wither before her eyes."I said hold it steady."

"But I thought—"

"I didn't ask you to think! I told you to hold it steady."

Robert grabs the tiller and brings the boat back on course. Jonathan slinks down into the cabin, but not before Marshall sees his eyes fill, and feels her own heart crumble with sorrow.

Olivia, on the other hand, had already accepted Robert as her father and before the evening was over, she behaved as though they'd never been apart. As he was leaving, Olivia had given him a big hug and a kiss on the cheek at the door. Marshall knew Robert would treasure that kiss tonight in his lonely hotel room.

"Daddy and I have so much catching up to do," Olivia had sighed when Marshall had gone to say good-night. "We're going to meet after school some time and just talk and talk. He'll pick me up and we'll go to a restaurant."

Marshall had laughed and stroked her daughter's

hair lovingly. "I hope you won't totally monopolize the conversation. He might have a few things to tell you, too."

"Bless your little heart," Marshall now whispered to the girl sleeping in the bedroom down the hall. "You've made your father so very happy."

Now if only Jonathan would try, even a bit . . .

Sleep. She had to stop thinking about all this or she would never survive in school the next day with her energetic pupils.

"Hey gorgeous!" Robert's voice over the phone was excited. "I finally have my launch date for my boat, so I'm going to the marina this weekend to clean her up. How about you come along and help me? I've done all the scraping and the hull's painted, but the cabin could use some feminine spit and polish."

"In other words you need a cleaning lady," Marshall stated.

"That just about covers it, yeah."

"And what do you mean by the weekend?" She suspected it meant exactly what she didn't want it to mean. "Are you planning to be there overnight?"

"Yes. Well, not exactly. That is . . . not necessarily."

There was a very pregnant pause, and Marshall knew he expected her to decline, but was trying his luck anyway.

"Unless you want to?" he added hesitantly.

She could hear the hope in his voice and didn't hesitate to crush it. "No, I don't want to."

With an audible sigh he went on. "It can be just for the day. My turn is at two o'clock. We'd have time to go for a short sail after the launch. So, will you come?"

Marshall put the phone against her breast while she

took a few deep breaths. Would that be wise? Of course it wouldn't. Did she want to go to the boat? Yes, of course she did. It had been so long since she'd last sailed, and the temptation was overwhelming.

"I don't know . . ." There were things to take into consideration, like being out on the lake in the intimate confines of a small boat with a man her body lusted after, and who felt the same. "I'd like to but—"

"Great!" Robert cried victoriously. "I thought I'd have to cajole you a lot more than this. I'll pick you up Saturday at eight. Try to be packed so we can hit the highway before the weekend cottagers fill it up."

"But I didn't—"

"You said you'd like to."

"I didn't mean it that way and you know it." But Marshall had to smile despite herself. Yes, Robert knew exactly what she meant.

And so a few days later, she was in Robert's silver Corvette speeding along the highway, heading north, away from the bustle of the city. When they got beyond the city limits, Marshall sighed with contentment. The rich black of the farmers' fields sported a soft mantle of green, and the trees displayed their newly unfurled, fragile leaves that were almost ready to fill the forests with lush greenery.

"How delicate and fresh all the colors are," Marshall said. "I love spring. Especially on a lovely day like this."

"So aren't you glad you decided to come?"

Marshall sighed. "Yes." No use denying it.

The sigh hid a fair amount of apprehension, but despite this, she tried to sit back and enjoy the morning. And as the barren rocks appeared along the highway—Jonathan had always called this area "Rockland"—Marshall felt a thrill of excitement surge through her. It was partly from seeing the familiar landscapes and partly from knowing she would soon be in a boat with Robert. Alone. The thought made her heart take a few quick flips.

After three hours of driving, they approached Georgian Bay, with its ancient bedrock, scraped bare by glaciers. Gnarled pines clung precariously to the scant soil and the pristine blue waters, dotted with idyllic islands, lurked with dangerous shoals. Marshall hadn't been there for years and had always missed it. Going there without Robert somehow just wouldn't have felt right.

Memories came flooding back and threatened to overwhelm her. Robert in his cut-offs, bare-chested, with a sun-browned leg casually slung over the helm, looking every bit like the handsome guy in a vacation ad, his dark, trim beard and wind-tousled hair adding charm to his wide, killer smile. What woman could resist that?

Well, she had to try. Not just try, but succeed. Because—she had to admit—the years had taken none of the edge off his charm and he was, if possible, even more attractive in a more mature way.

But then another memory forced itself into her brain and although she squeezed her eyes tight, it refused to be blocked off.

Robert is shaking a threatening fist at a passing speedboat, his beer can splashing its contents into the cockpit.

"Watch your wake, you fuckin' jerk! You're making my sails luff!"

He continues the drunken harangue as their sloop, Seagull, *wallows in the wake, the speedboat now far out of earshot.*

"Lookit! You made me lose the wind out of my sails! Stupid dickhead! I'll show you, you idiot!"

His shouts carry over the water to the nearby boats.

Mortified, Marshall ducks down into the cabin, knowing "the crazy drunk in Seagull*" will be the topic of conversation tonight at their marina club house. In the intimate boating community sailboats are easy to identify and the word gets around fast.*

Robert, oblivious to the turmoil inside her, placed a hand on her knee. His grin was infectiously happy.

"What makes this such a beautiful day is the fact that you're here beside me."

This gesture, plus the untarnished, clear blue sky helped to banish the troubling memories. Marshall wanted to enjoy this moment, for a sail on the beautiful bay with Robert—on one of his good days, of course—was something she had cherished. Too bad there hadn't been many of those over the years.

"I hope you brought enough woolens with you," Robert said. "It may be warm in the city, but when we get out on the bay it's a different world."

Marshall gave a short laugh. "No need to remind me. I'll never forget the day we sailed into the harbor wearing sweaters and tuques, after freezing our buns off all day on the water. And at the marina people were lounging on their boats in their swimsuits, perspiring in the heat and humidity. I felt like such a dork, when we peeled off our sweaters in front of the laughing spectators."

Robert chuckled. "I remember. But on to a more important subject. What did you bring for us to eat? When I carried the cooler into the car it felt nice and heavy. You do realize I asked you along so I'd get some decent food for a change?"

"What?" Marshall exclaimed. "Didn't you bring anything? I only brought enough for myself."

"You heartless joker. I'm sure you stuffed the cooler with great treats, like you always used to. Although the truth is, I brought you along so I could have a lovely woman in a bikini on board. All respectable yachts have a beautiful woman provocatively sprawled out on the deck."

"Only in advertisements. But a nice try, mister. I know you're just saying that to get food. Anyway, I didn't bring my bathing suit." But Marshall's vain feminine heart couldn't help fluttering at the thought that Robert imagined she would look good in a bikini. "Besides," she added, clearly fishing for a compliment, "I'm hardly the decoration I might have been years ago."

She accomplished her goal.

"Darling, I haven't seen you in a bikini . . . yet." Robert eyed her with a lustful sidelong glance. "But from what I've seen, I can tell you're as curvaceous as ever."

Marshall realized her vanity had led them into dangerous territory. And she had to admit ruefully, she'd done it on purpose. It was her own fault if he was now thinking about sex. Although . . . when wasn't he?

"So, what's the plan of attack for today?" she asked to sidetrack him.

"Well, we'll clean up a bit. Oil the teak and such. And once the boat is launched and the rigging's in place, we'll head out to one of the nearby island," Robert said. "We'll anchor there, have something to eat, and just relax before returning to the marina. We can have a late supper at the restaurant and then we'll drive back home."

"Sounds good." But his words set warning bells ringing in her head. Just relax—and do what? She was fully aware that although Robert had agreed to this "dating thing", he wasn't really committed to their agreement of "no sex". She knew it because she knew his sex drive only too well.

Which meant her guardian angel would have to do double duty to protect her from him, and from her own passions. Could she deny she was setting herself up on purpose? Being with him today in the intimacy of the boat was almost guaranteeing that she would find it impossible to resist him. And they might end up making love.

Making love with Robert at long, long last . . . She swallowed down the delicious desire that filled her mouth.

"Just remember, whenever we pass another yacht, you must strike an alluring pose and make the other captain green with envy."

"In my jeans and bulky sweater?"

"Yes, darling. You look sexy in anything."

Marshall sighed. "You're incurable."

They drove through the gates of the marina and Robert parked the car beside a large sailboat sitting in its cradle. *Wind's Way* was painted on the transom in cursive letters.

Marshall got out of the car. "So this is it." It was much like their *Seagull*, a full keel sloop with a sturdy tiller instead of a wheel.

She looked around her with interest. The whole yard was humming with people scraping, painting, varnishing and scrubbing with enthusiasm. Each spring she'd been a part of this bustle, and had loved every second of it.

Some boats were already afloat, lying in their slips, and some were still on land, sitting in their cradles or trailers, waiting to be set free. A huge lift was busily hoisting one boat after another into the water and a smaller crane was there to step the masts.

Robert got a ladder from under the keel and, setting it up against the hull, he gestured for her to go ahead. Marshall nimbly climbed up and stepped into the cockpit. He followed and as they stood there, for a few seconds time did a reverse-flip. It was spring, a long time ago, and they were on board their boat again after the long winter. What always followed was a warm hug, just holding each other, relishing the wonderful moment.

It seemed that Robert remembered the same thing, for he reached out from behind and wrapped his arms around her. And, despite her firm promises, Marshall couldn't prevent herself from leaning against his chest as a sigh of contentment rose from deep inside her. It felt so right, after all this time, to be here in his arms with the smell of the lake in her nostrils. But the moment didn't last. As his hands began to caress her and she quickly stepped out of his embrace.

"Are you going to let me see the interior?" she asked.

"Avec plaisir, madame." Robert dug out the key from the pocket of his jeans, undid the lock and pulled up the slides that covered the companionway. Marshall descended the three steps into the cabin.

It was set up much the same as their old boat had been, though this was slightly bigger. To the right were a navigation table, a book shelf, and a swivel chair attached to the floor. Across from that was the galley with a small propane stove, a fridge and a sink.

The main cabin had berths on either side with a

narrow table between them. Marshall knew the set up. They could be converted into a double bed in a snap, and the thought sent waves of nostalgia and sadness through her. She remembered the heady nights of love in the beginning, before the bottle had stolen her place as the love of his life.

Marshall ran the tips of her fingers along the smooth teak table top. She grimaced as a layer of dust appeared on her hand. "I kept *Seagull* much cleaner."

"Which is the reason I asked you to come along, remember? We can do a lot of damage before it's our turn to get launched."

So, with plenty of rags, buckets of water, teak polish and elbow grease they soon had the interior of *Wind's Way* sparkling.

"Time to relax," Robert sighed and threw himself onto the berth. "Could you get me a soft drink, please?"

"What am I? Your galley slave? Get it yourself and bring one for me, too, please." Marshall plunked herself down on the opposite berth, but when she stretched out her legs in the narrow cabin, one bare foot brushed against his thigh.

Robert took advantage of this by reaching to caress it.

Marshall drew her leg off to the side and frowned.
"Now I know why in the olden days women weren't allowed to show their feet. Some men can't control themselves at the sight of a woman's ankle."

"Some women have such alluring ankles that some men can't keep their hands off them," Robert riposted, and took a firm hold of hers. Then he also nabbed the other leg in a vice grip, making Marshall fall back against the cushions. She tried to kick, but he didn't let go. Instead he got up from his berth to tower over her.

"Robert, let go. Stop being silly." She half-laughed, half-scolded as the sense of being overpowered by him awakened as a sexual thrill inside her. She knew what would follow this kind of foolishness. "Let me go right now."

Robert didn't comply. He loomed above her and stepped closer between her legs, a sexy smile playing on his face.

She tried to sound angry. "Let me go, Robert. You're annoying me."

"Am I?" His hooded eyes, looking at her with obvious intent, caused her womb to convulse and sent a shiver of desire through her. He brushed her toes lightly against the front of his shorts, where the hardness made her gasp despite herself.

"Yes, you are." She marveled at how severe she was able to sound. Years of scolding little rascals, even when she would rather have laughed, had made her an expert in dealing with situations like this. Just like with this big rascal, playing dangerous games with her. Games that were on the verge of morphing into foreplay.

He stopped and regarded her for a moment, during which time she held her breath. Then, signaling his acquiescence with a shrug, he freed her ankles.

"Okay, our Miss Brooks," he said, letting her know that she hadn't fooled him with her severe teacher act. He stretched, as high as he could inside the cabin. "Shall we go for a stroll and see how thing are progressing in the yard?"

Marshall sat up, pretending enthusiasm. "Yes, let's." She put on her shoes and followed him out into the cockpit and down the ladder, all the while feeling perversely let down.

By the water's edge they watched the activity until it was their turn to get launched. The big lift came over to the boat, carried it off, and deposited it into the water. There, with the help from the smaller crane, the mast was stepped onto the deck. There was Wind's Way at last, floating in the water, where she was meant to be.

Marshall sighed. Just like she was meant to be in Robert's arms. But she pushed that thought into a far corner of her heart. Not yet. Maybe never, but definitely not yet.

They climbed aboard and Robert began to sort out the sheets.

Marshall held onto the stays that held the mast in place, while Robert tightened the attachments.

She shifted her weight from one foot to the other, to make the boat rock slightly under them. "I love the way she feels now. On the cradle she felt so hard and dead, but now there's life to her."

"Yes," Robert agreed. "There's give to her movement. And rhythm. Makes me think of a woman yielding to her lover."

Marshall frowned. "Shh."

Heads in the boat next to them turned and a grinning man raised his arm. "I'll drink to that!" he shouted.

Marshall turned her back on the fellow. Drink. That was one of the curses of sailors, and even the mention of it made her uneasy. Robert saluted the man and went on with his work.

Before long *Wind's Way* was motoring toward the open waters of Georgian Bay. As they left the marina behind, only the dull thunk-thunk of the diesel broke the late afternoon silence. Then Robert cut the engine and got ready to hoist the sails. It took Marshall a few moments to recall the steps of this operation, but she surprised herself and soon was hoisting the main sail as though she'd never been away from the job.

"Well, you caught on quickly again. I think I'll hire you back as a deck hand," Robert said.

"It's like biking. You never forget," Marshall replied. But the compliment made her blush with pride. She'd actually been a pretty good sailor back then, though she'd never dared to take their sloop out on her own.

Robert hoisted the foresail and soon the noisy flapping of the sails stopped as he set the boat to the wind. Marshall had always loved this moment. After the noisy, laboring engine was cut, the wind filled the sails and grabbed a hold of the boat, pushing it forward with a silent strength that awed her. The bow dipped and rose in a steady rhythm. There was something almost primeval about it—like the elemental movements of a man and woman engaged in the most natural act of all.

For Robert, having Marshall here with him again was like the fulfillment of an impossible dream. Whenever he had sailed alone—or even with another woman—he'd seen Marshall sitting there in the old familiar pose, like now, leaning her back against the bulkhead, arms wrapped around her knees, facing him as he sat at the helm. Now, as they sailed on, the years peeled away like so many layers of onion skin, until he was transported back to the very core of their happiness—together under the brilliant blue sky, the waves lapping against the hull. Every worrisome thing in the world was dissolved by the simple pleasure of being on the water, together.

"How about you go down and make me a cup of coffee?" he asks.

She raises her head from the pocket book she's reading. "Aw, why are you making me work so hard?"

"Because I need a coffee." He would rather have a beer, but knows she won't ever bring him one.

"Oh, okay, then, Simon Legree."

"And I want it brought to me by an alluring bikini-clad seductress!" he calls down after her.

"I'll see if I can find one down here."

A few minutes later she emerges, carrying a steaming coffee mug, wearing her red two-piece bathing suit.

She strikes a provocative pose and hands him the mug. "Okay?"

He takes a sip. "Great coffee. Thanks."

She pouts. "What about the alluring bikini-clad seductress?"

"What seductress? Where?" He looks around. "All I see is my old wife."

The pocket book smashes on his head, making him spill the coffee.

Robert laughed.

"What?" Marshall asked.

"Just thinking about the time you smacked me on the head with your book."

"That was funny?"

"Yeah. I thought it was."

The atmosphere in the cockpit was relaxed and few words broke the lazy peace of the afternoon. The small dinghy behind the boat made soft lapping sounds as it tugged at the end of its painter. Robert saw Jonathan in it, lying on his back reading a comic book, with his leg dangling over the side, trailing in the water.

He sighed, and right away Marshall's alert, questioning eyes turned to him. How he wished he could reel back time and have Jonathan little again. If only they could start over. Too bad life didn't allow a few rehearsals when you became a parent before you had to tackle the job for real. Once you were on stage it was live theatre all the way, and if you messed up, that was it. No retakes.

He glanced at the compass and moved the tiller slightly to make a correction. If only it were that easy to correct the mistakes in life.

But he'd been given another chance to make things right with Marshall and he wasn't going to mess that up. He winked at her, indicating that everything was all right, and her answering smile almost made him let go of the tiller and take her in his arms. That, of course, would have been a huge mistake. He knew her guard was up today against his advances, and he'd made up his mind to be on his "most goodest" behavior.

That sudden memory of Jonathan's baby talk caught him off guard and his eyes misted. For years he hadn't thought much about his son, not as a baby, nor as a youth, probably because he hadn't seen him for the past fourteen years. Or maybe because in the few years preceding the separation he hadn't been much of a father and had all but missed Jonathan's boyhood. Birthdays, Christmases, even sailing trips. Alcohol had obliterated so much that there weren't many events to remember. A groan escaped from deep inside him, which he tried to cover up with a cough.

Chapter Seven

After two hours of easy sailing, they anchored off an island and rowed ashore in the dinghy, with Robert at the oars and the cooler between Marshall's legs. He tied the painter around a tree trunk and then carried the cooler ashore.

Marshall contemplated the distance from the dinghy to the shore. Should she try to jump or step into the cold water?

Robert was watching her with a cynical expression on his face. "Do I have to help you out of the dinghy or can you still manage on your own?"

"Just watch me!"

Defiantly Marshall started to jump ashore but failed to take into account the movement of the dinghy and lost her footing. With a scream she landed in the shallow water on her hands and knees, with Robert's irritating laughter ringing in her ears.

"Stop cackling, you bastard!" she exploded. "Just because I'm out of practice—"

She began to get up, but the smooth, slippery rock

face beneath caused her to slip, and she ended up on her stomach in the water.

"You laugh any more and you won't get any lunch!" she fumed at him.

Robert put the cooler down and came to help her up.

"So you did bring something for me, too."

Marshall stood up, dripping wet and pulled off her wet t-shirt. She began to wring it out, but the very next minute she realized what she was doing and slapped the shirt against her breasts, where it clung to her like a second skin.

But it was too late. She saw the desire flash in Robert's eyes and knew he'd seen the dark nipples, puckered with cold, show through her wet, silky bra. Quickly she began to pull the shirt on over her head, but the wet fabric refused to co-operate. Robert took a step toward her while she struggled to push her hands through the armholes. He stopped within an arm's reach of her and she saw his Adam's apple rise as he swallowed.

"Are you trying to tempt me, sweetheart?" he asked hoarsely. "Because you should know it doesn't take much."

"No!" she cried hastily. "I'm not. For a second I just forgot."

Forgot this wasn't the old days. Forgot she wasn't free to expose herself to him. The whole day had brought back so many memories that undressing in front of him had seemed like the most natural thing to do. Something she'd always done. Almost in a panic Marshall turned her back on him and tugged and yanked to get her arms into the shirt.

She could hear his breathing as he approached her

from behind, and then his hands were on her shoulders. She shivered—not from the cold—as he gently turned her around. He took a hold of the tee and pulled it off over her head.

"We'll have to get you into something dry, or you'll be cold when the sun sets," Robert said.

She could see his hands shake as he fumbled with the clingy shirt wringing out more water. He then spread it out on a sunny rock. The whole time he hadn't touched her and Marshall wasn't sure if she was thankful or disappointed. She stood, hands covering her breasts like a virginal maiden.

"There's a few old duds in the cabin," Robert said, easing the tension. "I'll row back to the boat and get something for you. In the meanwhile you can get the food ready. I'm getting hungry." And with a wink he went to untie the dinghy.

On his return Marshall took off her bra, shorts and panties, making sure he was facing the lake. She wrung them out and hung them on branches to dry, replacing them with an old pair of Robert's sweatpants and a faded cotton shirt. The clothes were miles too big, but gave him an excuse to make jokes about her predicament.

Marshall knew he joked to cover up the feelings the sight of her almost naked state had aroused in him. When she thought about what her tumble into the water could have led to, she thanked her lucky stars for his unexpectedly gallant behavior.

After dinner they sat side by side, leaning back against a mossy boulder. Before them the lake glimmered in the dying light of the day and *Wind's Way* swung in a lazy arc in the gentle breeze. In the old days this would have been the time for a glass of wine, but now their happy hour consisted of the coffee Robert had made on the propane stove in the boat.

"Coffee by the water is almost as good as a glass of—" Guiltily Marshall bit off the sentence, but Robert had caught on.

"Wine." He stated firmly. "Say 'a glass of wine', darling."

"A glass of wine, darling," Marshall mimicked snarkily.

"You haven't been doing your homework," Robert admonished her. "You were supposed to keep repeating the word 'alcohol', remember?"

"But I have," Marshall insisted with an innocent face. "I just haven't been working on the word 'wine'."

"All right, Mrs. Smart-ass. Add wine and beer to your list, then. And vodka and brandy and whatever else you might want to say in front of me some day."

He put a hand on her neck as though to give her a shake, but at his touch she gasped, and all thought of joking vanished from her mind. She knew she must pull away, but she couldn't move, not even when his hand slipped down her back and drew her close to him. His other hand came around her waist and before she knew it, they were lying down on the soft pine needles. When his lips found hers she felt the ancient bedrock tremble beneath her. The kiss sent her mind spooling back the years, and no longer was she thinking of what should or shouldn't be happening. This was what she'd dreamed of for so long. She couldn't have stopped herself from kissing him back any more than the waves could stop from breaking against the shore.

"Marshall, my own darling," Robert whispered and settled himself between her legs that opened for him in the old, well-scripted way. "I've missed you so much. This is just like before. Like we've never been apart."

Just like before! The words jolted Marshall out of the sweet seduction, bringing her back from the brink of insanity. Pushing with all her might against his chest, she managed to roll away from under him.

She got up on her hands and knees. "No, Robert!" she cried hoarsely. "Don't you understand, it can't be like before!"

Slowly Robert sat up and raked both hands through his hair. "But it *was* like before. It doesn't seem to matter what we think it should or shouldn't be. It was like before. We love each other and sex is just one of the ways we express our love. As far as I'm concerned it's that simple. I want you and you would be lying if you tried to deny that you want me."

Marshall crouched down on the rock beside him. She wasn't going to let him win this one. "Of course I want you. But that isn't the point. The whole point of this is that we must do things differently this time around. We mustn't just jump into each other's arms and let sex anaesthetize us and make us forget the problems we have to deal with."

"Look," Robert put out a hand toward her. He desperately wanted her back in his arms, under his body like she'd been a minute ago. "My biggest problem right now is trying to figure out what our problem is." He knew his voice was too loud, too forceful, but he couldn't help it. His insides were roiling with the frustration of not being able to make love to her. "I don't drink any more. You've broken up with this Steve-fellow. I have no women hiding in my closet. Why can't we just get on with it? What's the hold-up?"

"The hold-up is figuring out how we solve our problems in the future when they inevitably arise—without resorting to sex. It's learning to be good parents to Olivia. The hold-up is Jonathan."

The words, pronounced low, sounded like a death-knell to his dreams. Olivia he could deal with. They seemed to have already hit it off. But what was he supposed to do about Jonathan? The boy—the man—was obviously not interested in starting any relationship with him. Not that he could blame his son because he hadn't been much of a father. In fact he hadn't been a father at all.

"What about Jonathan?" A stupid question. He was playing for time.

"I can't stand the thought that the two men I love most in the world are ready to throw daggers at each other whenever they're in the same room. What would that do to our Christmases? To birthdays? I'm not about to go through the rest of my life living in two camps, yours and Jonathan's, and I certainly don't want every family get-together spoiled by the two of you."

"Yes, just think of how that could throw a wet blanket on some great-aunt's funeral."

Marshall sprang up and Robert knew he'd just blown it big time.

She stood above him like an avenging angel. "Make fun of it if you wish!" she shouted furiously. "But I will not live my life like that! I will *not*!"

With determined steps she walked to the edge of the water and Robert could see her shoulders heaving. Then she turned to face him and wiped the tears from her cheeks.

"I've lived a peaceful life since our separation and

divorce," she began, her tremulous voice sending a shaft of pain through his heart. "It hasn't been the wonderful, happy life we had at the beginning of our marriage, but after all the horror we went through, the peace has been a godsend. I told you I will not go back to that life with you again."

"But I don't drink any more." Yes, he knew that wasn't the problem she'd been talking about, but compared to the father-son conundrum, winning the battle with the bottle now seemed like a cake walk. At least in dealing with his alcoholism he'd been in charge, and he hadn't had to consider how anyone else felt about things. But of course, after he'd lost everyone what did it matter how anyone else felt.

Marshall looked at him severely, almost making him squirm like a naughty schoolboy. She had a way about her when she put on that stern teacher face. He sat, arms resting on his knees, and sighed in resignation.

"Okay. What do you want me to do?"

"Speak to him. Make some gesture of reconciliation. He'll respond, I'm sure." Already she sounded hopeful, just because he'd asked the right question.

But Robert knew better. Any overture would be thrown back at him as fast as it was offered. He'd seen the boy's stony face at dinner, shut tight against him, and he knew prying it open would be about as easy as trying to break into Fort Knox.

Robert shook his head. "I don't think he'll—" But he stopped when he saw her face cloud up again. He couldn't take that. Making her happy and keeping her from any more pain was now the absolute goal in his life. He would do anything to achieve that.

"All right, why don't I give it a shot," he said and almost choked up when he saw how her face brightened at his words. She'd always been like that, grabbing at any errant ray of sunshine and making a bright day out of it. He ran a hand across his eyes to wipe away the moisture and then held it out to her.

"Come here, Marshall. Let's just sit here and watch the sun go down. Then we'll start back for the marina. I remember how you always loved sailing at night, with all the buoys and lighthouses and harbor lights blinking in the dark."

She moved toward him hesitantly.

"I won't do anything, I promise."

"Yes, like you promised before," she said with a small pout, but she continued to advance slowly like a shy child, while he continued to hold out his hand.

"I know. And I can't apologize for it, because it all just happened so fast. I don't even know how we suddenly got into that rather—uh—compromising position with me lying between your legs." He stopped to swallow down the desire that rose into his mouth at the thought. "From now on my promises are only for each separate situation. I'm not promising never to touch you the entire length of this dating relationship."

"I wouldn't want you to," she almost whispered, and sent a huge tidal wave of hope crashing through him.

And then, at last, she was where he wanted her, sitting beside him again, leaning her head on his shoulder as the sun began its slow descent into the darkening waters.

"Please put your arm around me," she said. "I'm getting cold."

Robert was eager to comply. "Better?" Gently he stroked her hair.

"Yes. Much better."

After a while she said, "I think we did it."

"Did what, darling?"

"We had an argument and we talked about it and we came to a compromise."

"We did?" He had no idea what she was talking about.

"We argued about what to do about Jonathan, and instead of getting all furious, you agreed to speak with him. That would never have happened in the old days. You would have yelled at me and stomped off and been mad for days."

"I would?"

"Yes. And given me the silent treatment."

She was right. He used to do that, but in the future he would try his damnest not to cause her any more unhappiness. As much as possible he wanted to make up for all those years when he'd given her grief. "Maybe the reason I didn't stomp off is because we're on an island?"

She laughed. "So actually this wasn't the successful experiment I thought it was. I guess we'll have to see what happens when another situation arises."

"Darling, I don't think you'll ever again see me behave like that. My whole purpose for living now is to make you happy. Trust me."

She was silent for so long he thought she'd dozed off. "Trust you?" she spoke at last. "How can I know you won't again choose the vodka bottle over me?"

Damn! He wished she hadn't asked that question, because he didn't have an answer. He held her tight and pressed his face against her hair. "Darling, all I can say is that I'll keep trying till my dying day to never choose anything or anyone over you."

She looked up at him and his heart swelled with love. "But the one promise I can make with no reservations, with no hesitation, is that I'll love you forever."

Marshall smiled up at him and he hoped his words had given her some measure of comfort and security. The two things she'd told him she wanted in life.

"So will you come for dinner next Sunday?" she asked quietly, sending his mood plummeting down to his toes along with his stomach.

A week later Robert dutifully rang the doorbell of Marshall's townhouse. The door was opened by Olivia, whose happy face failed to dispel his nervousness.

"Daddy!" the girl cried and immediately gave him a hug, and a kiss on the cheek. Robert tried to enjoy this sincere affection, knowing a different kind of welcome awaited him from his son.

Robert wished he could have had something stronger than a soft drink, but it was just moments like this that he'd been training himself to face throughout his recovery.

Olivia's cheerful chatter kept his nerves from unraveling, while Marshall made the final dinner preparations in the kitchen.

The wait for Jonathan was on.

At last Robert heard his son's voice at the front door. Heard it only too well, unfortunately.

"So what's the big event I have to make a command appearance for this time?" Jonathan obviously made no effort to lower his voice. "You two going to announce your engagement or something?"

"Shh. Don't be impertinent, Jonathan. Your father's here."

Sorry, Marshall, that wasn't quiet enough. Robert's stomach tightened up. Although the aroma of food had been deliciously tempting just a few minutes ago, he didn't think he now would be able to eat a single morsel.

"Yeah, I know. I saw his fancy wheels on the driveway." Jonathan's voice was disparaging.

Fancy wheels. For chrissake, the boy had to put down even his car.

Jonathan stepped into the family room where Olivia was cozily seated beside Robert on the couch, one leg under her, one arm crooked on Robert's shoulder.

"Ah, what a picture of family bliss," Jonathan quipped—almost sneered—and took a snapshot with an imaginary camera.

Robert tried to go along with the joke. "All we need is the mother and the son," he said with a grin that he knew was much too jovial. "And the whole family will be in the picture."

"Yeah. That's all we need for everything to be hunky-dory again."

The steely glint in Jonathan's eyes sent a chill down Robert's back. It would be impossible to break through this barrier and keep his promise to Marshall. But he had to try. For Marshall's sake, he had to do his best, and he could only hope it would also be for Jonathan's sake.

The dinner proceeded quite well, Marshall thought. Robert was more communicative this time than during the previous dinner. Not that he spoke to Jonathan more than a couple of times in a general sort of way about sports or whatever, but it was a start.

But it made her heartsick to notice that Jonathan's words were never directed at his father. Not once. If only she'd kept quiet about the "conciliatory gesture", because obviously Jonathan wasn't ready for anything of that sort. Maybe in a few months—or years—he might warm up to his father, but tonight was definitely not the time for it.

Marshall wanted to pull Robert aside and give him the "abort" signal, but it was too late. She'd just brought out the dessert when she realized to her horror that Robert had chosen this moment to speak up.

"So, Jonathan," Robert began in the kind of voice that one uses with a little buddy. Mistake number one. Marshall froze and her eyes went to Jonathan's face and stayed there, glued to his closed, almost hostile expression. Robert was heading for a crash landing and she didn't know how to prevent it.

"I got a couple of tickets to the baseball game on Friday night. I'd really like it if you came with me."

As he forced the words out, Marshall could feel, inside her own body, the tightness that she knew was knotting his gut. He was vying for a comradely tone, but it came out too loud and much too chummy. Failure was written all over this scene and it was her fault for pressuring him into it. Her heart bled for him.

Jonathan looked directly at his father and, without blinking, he said, "Sorry, I'm busy."

"Another night then?" Robert pursued.

Stop! Stop! Marshall wanted to screamed outloud.

"I don't think so."

For a moment the father and son looked at each other, silently communicating their hostilities.

Robert put down his fork. "I think I've had enough. Thanks." With firm steps he walked into the family room and Marshall knew he wasn't referring to the dessert.

"But, dad, this is so good!" Olivia cried after him.

"Mom said she was making it especially for you because apple pie with cheese used to be your favorite. And you hardly had any."

"It's very delicious, but I think I had too much main course," Robert replied from the family room. "Thanks for making it, though." The last comment was directed at Marshall, and lacked the endearment she'd begun to expect.

Olivia went into the family room to keep him company while Marshall escaped into the kitchen with a load of dirty dishes.

Jonathan followed her. "I'll help you with the dishes," he offered.

But Marshall was too angry with him to want his help, or even have him near her. "I'm putting everything in the dishwasher," she said brusquely.

"The pots and pans you always do by hand. I'll dry them for you," Jonathan persisted. He obviously was looking for an excuse to keep away from his father.

He picked up a tea towel, while Marshall squirted liquid detergent into the sink. She turned on the tap, which also seemed to release Jonathan's tongue.

"Mom," he said in a subdued voice. "If he stops bugging me with that father-son shit, I'll tolerate his presence in your life. But only because you're my mother and I love you."

Marshall felt all strength drain from her and she leaned against the counter for support.

"I'm sorry, Jonathan, but that's not enough for me. I already told your father I can't live like that. I won't be in two camps, and I also won't put up with this kind of hellish tension whenever you two are together. I'm greedy and I want all or nothing." She turned off the tap and slowly began to scrub a pot.

"What does that mean, exactly?" He gave the counter a wipe while waiting.

"It means that since I can't have my family together, then I won't consider getting together with your father. We'll go back to the way things were before he came into our lives. Steve said he would wait for me, though I told him he shouldn't." The thought almost made her burst into sobs and laughter at the same time, but she held on. "We'll pick up our lives where we left off."

She continued scrubbing and waited for Jonathan's reaction which was slow in coming.

"You don't love Steve," he said at last. He ran a hand through his hair and spoke slowly, almost as if he were pondering a new concept.

Marshall decided to be blunt. "No, I don't. Not like I love your father."

He twisted the dish towel into a knot. "So you won't be happy then."

She continued to scrub with vigor. "I'll be happier than in this hostile environment. It's a trade-off." But she felt as though she was scrubbing out her last chance for real happiness in this life. "I'll tell your father tomorrow."

They finished the pans in a strained silence.

"No, we're not calling it quits!" Robert yelled. "I'll never give you up, not if I have to crawl on my hands and knees in front of that god-damned kid!"

Marshall had known his reaction would be violent.

Olivia wasn't home from school yet, but Robert had come over after school, "just because". She knew exactly how he felt because after not seeing him for a few days it was like something vital was missing from her life.

Yet somehow she had found the strength to tell him she couldn't stand the hostility between him and Jonathan. It was almost as big a strain on her nerves as his drinking had been.

"He's not a god-dammed kid," she said angrily. The mother in her was furious with Robert for saying such things about her son. About his son. She restrained herself with great difficulty. "Jonathan is just very, very angry with you for letting him down when he needed you. You can't blame him for that."

They were in the kitchen and Marshall was getting dinner started. Or trying to, because the tense atmosphere in the room made it impossible for her to recall what ingredients she needed for the stew.

There was a long silence, followed by a very audible sigh. "I know. You're right. I have to apologize to him."

The quiet words made her heart go out to him. "I don't think he's ready for apologies at this point, Robert. Maybe one of these days, after he's got used to you being around."

Her inadvertent choice of words had a visibly uplifting effect on him. "Well, that means I'll have to stick around then, doesn't it?" Robert said jubilantly. "Calling it quits at this stage would be premature."

Marshall had to admit that she was happy that her decision to end the dating had so summarily been waylaid. She didn't want to call it quits. And although she'd told Jonathan that she would go back to Steve, there was no way on earth she could do that after being with Robert. Kissing Steve? Having sex with him? Never again. Not because Steve was an incompetent lover, but because after being with Robert again, it was simply unthinkable.

"Yes, I guess it means you'll have to stick around,"

she said, and although her head was in the fridge where she was picking out carrots and an onion from the vegetable crisper, she knew he could hear the smile in her voice.

"But let's go easy on the family dinners," he said. "I don't know if I can take any more of them."

She handed him a bag of potatoes and a peeler. "I'm sure Jonathan feels the same way. And, as a matter of fact, I'll be a lot happier, too, without all that strain."

Robert began to peel the potatoes over the sink. "So, when's our next date? I can't be too long without you, you know. Without your love I'll wither away and die."

"Oh, how melodramatic!" Marshall laughed. "You're with me now, aren't you?"

"This isn't the same as being with you somewhere private. Like a dark movie theatre or in my car. I think we'll go dancing next. That'll give me a chance to hold you all evening."

Marshall wanted to laugh with joy. No, she wasn't ready to give up Robert, because since he'd come back into her life, she felt like she finally was alive again. It was as though all these years she'd merely been existing, waiting for someone to come and take her home again. And now that he had come, she didn't want to turn back to an existence without him.

Just the other day she and Kelly had been eating their bagged lunches in a reasonably quiet, sunny corner of the schoolyard, keeping an eye on the kids who were playing on the climber.

Marshall laid her lunch bag on her lap. "You know, all these years away from Robert I think I've just been waiting," she mused thoughtfully.

Kelly took a sip of coffee from a thermos cup. "What do you mean? Waiting for what?"

"It's like for the past fourteen years I've only been going through the motions of living, of being a mother, of being a teacher. All that time I was actually just waiting to go back to my real life, before Robert and I separated. Nothing has been real since then, you know."

"I understand," Kelly had replied. "I think."

But whether Kelly understood or not, Marshall was thankful her friend hadn't made her feel like she was crazy. She pulled out a sandwich.

"It's kind of strange, but one day I just suddenly became aware of the fact that for so many years I haven't really been living. It happened maybe a year ago when I was driving home from visiting a friend out in the country. I was admiring the lovely scenery around me and thinking how kind and good-natured Steve always was, and how lucky I was to have found such a man after the turmoil of my life with Robert.

"But all of a sudden this strange feeling came over me. It was as though I was watching everything from the outside. Like I was standing backstage in the wings, waiting for my cue to come back on stage and pick up my lines where I'd left off. The person on stage with Steve was just pretending to be me and she was fooling everyone. The show that was being played was all wrong. The real me was standing there in the wings, trying to figure out what happened to the show I used to be in. The one where Robert starred with me."

"I certainly never noticed anything different about you," Kelly had said, making it obvious that her friend didn't really have a clue what Marshall was talking about, and was just trying to be helpful. Maybe trying to make her feel the stuff she was blabbering wasn't totally idiotic.

"When I got home I looked at everything in the house with new eyes. This wasn't my home. My home had a family with a husband and two kids, but this house only has a lonely mother and a daughter. And this wasn't my yard. My yard had a long run for Amber in the back, but this yard doesn't even have a dog, because Amber is dead. The poor thing died, still missing her master."

And now she felt the house was home again, because she was with Robert, where she belonged. She wasn't standing in the wings any more. She was back on stage and the play was the right one, starring Marshall and Robert.

Marshall wiped the tears surreptitiously from her eyes as she peeled the carrots. No, she wasn't ready to give him up, nor their life together. She knew she was a fixer—always had been—which was the reason she'd stayed so long with Robert, trying her best to save the alcoholic and their marriage. Of course she'd failed.

But she didn't want to fail now. Somehow she had to get Jonathan and his father to make up, because getting them to live in peace was the only way she, herself, would ever be happy again. Maybe she was being too selfish, too greedy, but she had to try.

"Hey, Earth to Marsh! Earth to Marsh! Are you there? I asked if I should cube the potatoes."

"You bet I'm here," she said with a catch in her voice. "And yes, cube the potatoes into small chunks and put them into this pot. And going dancing would be nice," she added.

"Well, what a coincidence! My client up in Bracebridge is having a little party this weekend to celebrate the completion of the plaza we've been building for him," Robert said, chopping the potatoes with vigor. "I was going to go by myself, but if you came with me, I could make an appearance and we could have our dance date. Kill two birds with one shot."

He dumped the cubed potatoes into the pot and rinsed his hands under the faucet. Then with both hands he flipped the hand towel over her head and pulled her against him. "Whaddya say, huh?

Marshall gave a little scream of surprise at the sudden move and then leaned against his chest. He shifted her into a dance hold and started to waltz her from the kitchen out into the family room.

"One, two three, one two three, you look so good to me," he sang in his deep baritone and spun her around and around.

He'd always been a good dancer and obviously still was. His firm hand on her back, guiding her, made Marshall feel like a young girl again. And although she hadn't danced a waltz for over two decades, she still moved lightly on her toes, easily following his lead.

"Marshall, you dance like a feather!" Robert said.

The compliment, plus the speed of the whirling dance were enough to make her lose her equilibrium and she stumbled.

They stopped. "I take that back. You dance like an old cow."

"What!" Marshall yelped. "How dare you say such a thing to a woman you are trying to woo?"

"I dare because it shows I love the woman even if she dances like an old cow." He nuzzled her neck. "And I'll love her when she's old and wrinkled and her hands look like your mother's did."

"Like two cans of worms?"

"Exactly. I'll kiss them every day and caress them." He proceeded to do just that. "And I'll massage heat ointment on them to ease the pain of her rheumatism."

"Thank you. And I'll do the same for you."

"Except I'm not planning to have rheumatism in my hands. But I always appreciate a massage somewhere else on my body."

Marshall escaped from his arms. "I will not be drawn into that kind of nonsense! I know exactly where it will lead."

"I only wish." He glanced at his watch. "But since Olivia is due home soon, it won't lead anywhere. However, I do expect you to keep your promise to come to the party with me."

Marshall returned to the kitchen to restart the interrupted stew preparations and Robert followed her. "What promise?' she asked."I don't remember promising to go with you to Bracebridge."

"You poor dear. Your short-term memory is already going," he said and picked up an onion from the counter." Of course you promised."

She handed him a celery stick. "Chop and shut up," she told him and turned to the sink to hide her smile.

"So I'll pick you up at four on Saturday. The cocktails are at six. It's a semi-formal."

Chapter Eight

Robert looked breathtakingly handsome in his tuxedo. When Marshall met him at the door, he whistled, stoking her feminine vanity and making her feel desirable. In his eyes she saw a dangerous glint that sent shivers of anticipation down to the pit of her stomach. Yes, she knew her dress was seductive, and she was asking for it, but a defiant voice inside her hurtled a dare to the fates. Tonight she wanted to flaunt her sexuality! She'd bought the dress just days ago with that very purpose in mind, so she had no one but herself to blame for his reaction.

Robert pinned a corsage of coral roses to her dress.

"You remember I like coral roses." Marshall gulped back a sob, moved by his gesture. "I'm extremely impressed by your memory."

"Thanks. I know it's funny I should remember that, even though the last years of our marriage I never gave you flowers of any kind. And for that I will be forever sorry." He helped on her wrap. "I knew damned well even if I'd brought you a daisy from the roadside, it would've made you happy. I knew that, but refused to do it. You didn't deserve flowers because you disapproved of my drinking." He kissed the back of her neck.

The kiss sent shivers down her back. "Yes, a daisy would have been very welcome, coming from you. But that's water under the bridge, so we won't talk about it any more." She sniffed the flowers. "This lovely corsage makes up for all that."

"For all that? You're too easily appeased, my darling. To make up for all those years I neglected you, I promise you'll always have fresh flowers in the house as long as I'm alive."

Marshall shook her head. "Wow! That's a huge order. When can I expect these floral deliveries to begin?"

"The day we're married," Robert replied. His voice was now firm and serious, with no hint of playfulness.

It sent streams of hope flowing through her. Would it really come to that? It sounded scary and joyful at the same time and she didn't know whether to cry or rejoice at the thought.

Olivia came down to see them off. "Have a lovely evening, children," she sang out. "And don't stay out past your curfew."

Robert gave her a kiss on the cheek. "Don't wait up for us, sweetie. We may not even make it home tonight.

"Ooo!" Olivia howled suggestively.

"There's nothing to 'Ooo' about, my dear!" Marshall tried to sound disapproving. "It's a two-hour drive to Bracebridge. That's all your father means."

"No, I don't," Robert put in, feigning innocence. "That's not what I meant."

By now Olivia was doubled over with laughter. Marshall snorted at her disdainfully and marched out the door.

"That was totally inappropriate," she scolded him when they got in his car. "We're not even married."

"But we will be, and Olivia has to get used to the fact that we love each other and have a healthy sex life." He sighed. "Or I trust we will have a healthy sex life, whenever we get around to it."

"Which will not be tonight." But deep inside her a tiny voice was telling her she was a hopeless hypocrite. If she didn't want to entice him, why had she bought this dress?

Two hours later they entered the reception room. The party was at the local resort, a posh establishment, more than slightly out of Marshall's snack bracket. People were milling around the bar, the band was playing, and some brave souls were already on the dance floor.

"Would you like a drink?" Robert asked, indicating with his head toward the bar.

"I'd really rather dance first," Marshall told him. She'd been looking forward to this evening like a little kid to a birthday party.

A new piece was just starting—the slow "Unchained Melody".

Robert bowed. "Your wish is my command." He put his arm around her waist and led her to the floor.

"O, my love, my darling," the soloist crooned. The words brought a lump to Marshall's throat and when Robert looked down at her, she made no effort to hide the tears in her eyes.

His arm tightened around her. "Darling," he groaned. "I have hungered and I have ached for your touch a terribly long and lonely time. Much too long."

The emotion inside him was revealed by the

moisture in his eyes.

Marshall brought her hand up to caress his cheek. "So have I," she whispered. Why try to deny it?

Robert turned his head to kiss her palm and then wiped the tears from her face with his thumb. "Look at us," he said with a soft chuckle. "Aren't we a pair? Came here to have a good time and both end up crying."

"But it's a good kind of crying," Marshall said. "It releases the tension."

"Right, teacher, but it's not doing much to release the tension I feel somewhere else when you're in my arms and I know I can't make love to you."

Of course she'd known this topic would come up. The evening was perfectly set up for it, but still she tried to dodge the inevitable. "Don't go there, Robert."

"With you dressed to kill? You must be kidding! I wouldn't be alive if I didn't feel anything."

"My bad," Marshall admitted with a little rueful smile. "But I just wanted to see if I still have it."

"You got it, baby. Never doubt it."

With a sigh Marshall snuggled against his chest as the singer continued to wring more emotions from deep within her. And she knew Robert felt the same. She could feel his heart beat faster as he held her close and hid his face against her neck.

When the dance was over Robert shook himself. "Whew! That was one emotion-packed number." He led her across the floor to introduce her to his client, a short, slightly rotund, balding man in his early fifties.

"Mrs. Kenton," the man gushed, taking her hand. "I must tell you what a great pleasure it has been working with your husband. Everything was finished on time, or even ahead of schedule, and the workmanship is fifteen out of ten. Every detail has been looked after."

"I'm so glad to hear that," Marshall said. She turned to Robert. "You didn't tell me you had such an appreciative client."

"And Robert didn't tell me he had such a charming wife," the man said. "Robert, you should have introduced us months ago. I would have had you over for dinner. Though I can't say I blame you if you want to keep her to yourself."

Robert laughed politely. "Thanks, George. I like to keep her in the kitchen. I don't bring her out too much in public."

"Shame on you. But I must have a dance with you, Mrs. Kenton," George said.

"Marshall," she told him. "My name is Marshall." As always, she exaggerated the "l" at the end of her name to make sure people didn't think she was saying Marsha.

"Marshall? Such a different name for a woman, if you don't mind me saying so," George said. "I find it exudes strength."

"Thanks, I like that. It's courtesy of my grandmother, who got it from her grandmother. It seems to skip a generation, like some genetic medical condition."

They all laughed at that.

"Our daughter isn't burdened by it," Marshall went on, "but she may decide it's a perfect name for *her* daughter. We'll see when the time comes."

"May I?" George asked with a slight bow, and soon Marshall was led away by him, while her heart stayed behind with Robert. When they danced by him, Robert winked at her and she pushed out her lower lip in a pout.

As she danced the slow piece with George, she saw Robert talking with some of the guests. Then, to her consternation, they moved toward the bar and she could see him ordering something. A drink.

Her heart plummeted. She wanted to rush over and prevent him from drinking it. Would this damned dance never end? George was making small-talk to which she paid no attention and only responded with nods and smiles, which seemed to satisfy him. Every cell in her body was beamed toward the bar where Robert was standing, chatting, holding a glass of red wine. She saw him raise it, just as George whirled her away and she lost her line of vision. The sinking feeling inside her weighed her down and she had to force her feet to keep moving.

The music went on and on while Marshall sweated with anxiety. Since this number had brought out so many couples, the band had obviously decided they should prolong it ad infinitum and keep the customers happy.

At last she couldn't take it any longer. She gave George a sweet smile. "The band seems to have their needle stuck in a groove," she said. "Should we go and join the others?"

"Of course." George led her to the bar where Robert was standing with his drink.

"Your wife is a fabulous dancer," George enthused.

"She's not bad," Robert agreed. "It's taken me a few years but I think she's finally mastered the steps."

George's laughter boomed loudly. He thanked Robert and gave Marshall a small bow before walking off to join the other guests.

Marshall stood stiffly. Fourteen years ago she'd

vowed she would never again put up with his drinking and here she was, anger bubbling out of every pore. She couldn't believe Robert would fall back into his old ways with their dating hardly begun. He had to be pretty sure he had her hooked. Or maybe he'd lied to her and he hadn't been sober for nine years as he claimed.

And then Robert handed her the glass he'd been holding. "Honey, I got you a merlot while you were dancing. I'll just grab a ginger ale and we can go out on the terrace and look at the sunset, like they do in those romantic movies you like to watch."

Luckily Robert had already turned and didn't see how her trembling hand almost made the wine spill. The aftershock was hitting her and she couldn't stop shaking. What an idiot she was! She'd almost brought herself to the brink of collapse by not trusting him.

Never again. Never again would she doubt him without reason. She took a deep breath and blew it out to calm herself before Robert returned, carrying his ginger ale. With his arm around her waist, they walked out to the terrace where the sun was just getting ready to set over the golf course. A pond in the distance sparkled with a rainbow of brilliant jewels.

"Reminds me you should dig out those rings from wherever you've got them stashed, because I'd like to see an engagement ring glitter here very soon." He took her left hand and caressed her ring finger. "Or are you thinking you'd like a new one?"

"You're feeling pretty sure about how this whole thing will work out, aren't you?" Marshall said. The horrible sinking feeling was gone and she felt like flying.

"Yes, I am. Aren't you?"

"I wish I could be, but, no I'm not."

"Because . . .?"

"Because of Jonathan." And because of the doubts that had never completely left her.

Robert placed his glass on the flat railing, took hers and did the same. Then he took her in his arms. "Marshall, let's not talk about Jonathan tonight. Let's pretend there's no one else in the world but just the two of us." He brushed her forehead lightly with his lips. "Could we? Just tonight? A bit of play-acting, making believe we're lovers, the way we used to be."

"That's silly," Marshall began, but then it hit her. "Lovers? What exactly are you thinking?"

"I'm thinking exactly what you think I'm thinking. Olivia doesn't expect us home tonight, and—"

Marshall trembled. She knew he felt it and she stepped away. "But that was just joking."

He looked into her eyes. "Was it?" His voice was a growl.

She avoided his eyes and gave a short, confused laugh. "Of course. I never thought—"

"Never?" He ran his palms down the sides of her figure-hugging, sexy-on-purpose dress.

He had her there. Of course she had every intention of seducing him, but she hadn't thought it would come quite this far. Or had she?

"Marshall, just for tonight. It would only be an interlude. A moment away from reality, like people who have a love affair on a cruise."

She swallowed. It would only be pretending. Just for tonight. God, why was she even considering it? She had no intention of going through with this. "This is silly," she said but her voice had a wobble that she couldn't hide. And which he, of course, caught.

"Rooms have been booked here for all the guests. We'll go to mine for the night and pretend it's twenty years ago."

"No!" she tried to sound angry. "That's not going to happen."

"Darling, I know you want me just as much as I want you. We'll have just this one night of love and then tomorrow we'll go back to holding hands."

"This is crazy." She had a hard time getting the words out. Maybe because what she really wanted to say was, "yes".

"Please, Marshall? Make love with me tonight." His head came down, his lips almost touching hers. "Just tonight," he whispered.

She wanted him. She was hungering for him. With a moan she raised her mouth to his and her fingers tangled into his hair.

The kiss was deep and passionate. Marshall clung to him like she could never get close enough. And she could feel him wanting her just as desperately.

The sound of chairs scraping and the ring of cutlery made Marshall aware of their surroundings. Reluctantly she broke away.

"Sounds like they're going to be serving dinner," Robert said, his voice thick. "I guess we should go to our seats."

But dinner was the last thing she wanted right now.

They took the hotel elevator up to their floor. As soon as they stepped out into the hall, Robert whisked Marshall up in his arms. "Let me carry you to our secret love nest, princess."

"Shh! Everyone is sleeping," she whispered with a giggle. "The room number is 732. You're going the wrong way."

"Oh no!" He made a quick u-turn. "I'm wasting precious time here."

"We have all night," she comforted him and stroked the back of his neck, making it even more urgent for him not to waste a single second.

For fourteen long years he'd wanted her, needed her every night, and now she was here in his arms. During all those years he'd imagined what he would do if he ever had a chance to make love to her again. And now that unbelievable moment was here.

Still carrying Marshall in his arms, Robert fumbled with the entry card, sticking it in backwards, then upside down in his hurry.

"Damn card. It's defective," he grumbled. But at last the green light flashed and saved him from going down to the front desk with a full erection to ask for a new card.

The room had one king bed and it was toward this that Robert now aimed his steps, after kicking the door shut behind him. He placed her carefully on the bed and started to remove his tie. "First I undress, and then I undress you. How does that suit you?"

Marshall lay on the bed, an arm behind her head in a very alluring pose. "Sounds like a plan. I'll let you do all the work. I'm too tired."

He quickly unbuttoned his shirt. "Oh no, you can't be."

"I am. I'll probably fall asleep right in the middle of it all."

But he could see her eyes growing dark with desire. "Keep looking at me and you won't fall asleep. My fabulous sexy body will make you squirm with longing."

He unzipped his pants and let them drop to the floor, along with his boxers, all the while holding her with his eyes. He felt such an incredibly tender love for her that he had to stop and just take in the wonder of having her there. All thought of joking was gone. He bent down and gently kissed her face.

"I love you, Marshall," he whispered and brushed a strand of hair from her face. "I love you more than I could ever imagine loving anyone."

He slid his hands down her body, and through the silky dress he could feel all her lovely curves. She turned herself over to one side so he could undo the long zipper down her back. After this the dress peeled off easily and then she was there, lying on the bed in her lacy bra and panties just waiting. All ready for him.

"You put these on for me, didn't you?" he asked huskily, fingering the soft fabric of the bra.

"Yes," she whispered.

He removed the bra, and she raised her hips so he could pull off the panty. This movement almost made him lose it. All his plans of taking it slowly, savoring every moment, flew out the window and he only wanted to bury himself inside her. And from the way her tongue licked over her lips, he knew she had the same need.

But for a few more moments he still wanted to just stare at her, take in her lovely body, remember every curve, every blemish, every little mark.

Under his intense scrutiny she seemed to grow hesitant. "I'm older now," she said, "Not like—"

He silenced her with his mouth. "You're just as beautiful as when I first saw you naked," he said. "I wouldn't want anything different."

She sighed. "Me neither."

He kissed her then, deeply and searchingly, tasting the wine she'd had with dinner on his tongue. But the only desire this roused in him was to have more of her. As his hands wandered over her body, she moaned her pleasure, making his arousal grow even harder, if that was possible.

And then he couldn't wait any longer. He was about to enter her, when suddenly her eyes snapped open.

"What about a condom?" she cried in a panic.

Robert groaned in frustration. "Honey, I've been protecting myself each and every time I've had sex, so you won't get anything from me. And as far as you're concerned, I don't care if you give me syphilis. I just want you."

"I've also had protec—"

Robert put a hand to her mouth. "I don't want to hear about it. I want to pretend you've always been mine. Only mine."

"Yes, I have always been yours," she murmured. "Only yours."

"And for me there has never been anyone but you," he said. Because in his heart there never had.

He came into her slowly, as though he were entering some sacred place, because that was what she was to him. She was his to worship with his body. Just like it had said in their wedding vows.

But after a while her movements told him she was ready for more forceful loving, and he quickened his rhythm until she was whimpering under him.

And then, as always, she took him with her to a wild, frantic release. They clung to each other as wave after wave of almost unbearable pleasure shot through him. The same mid-blowing ecstasy they'd always shared, ever since the early days when they had been learning how to please each other.

Afterwards, he propped himself up on one elbow, and looked down at her as she lay beside him, her face glowing with love. Love for him! He couldn't believe she was there. That they had just made love. That this wasn't just another dream he would wake up from. And weep.

"Darling," he murmured. "If you look at me like that I think I'm going to cry."

"I just love you so much," she whispered.

"I don't deserve to be this happy."

Robert knew that vodka could never compare with this. When temptation came, he would think about her loving face, about making love to her, and that would be enough to make him resist the urge to drink.

At least he hoped it would.

"Jonathan, let's leave the dishes till later," Marshall said. "Please come out for a walk with me. I'd like to talk to you."

Jonathan was visiting after work on a week night, something he did whenever his fridge was empty. He'd just finished wolfing down the shepherd's pie and was carrying his plate to the sink.

Watching him eat, Marshall had made the sudden decision that tonight would be it.

"You can't talk to me in the house?" Jonathan asked, glancing wistfully at the TV where a baseball game was starting. Obediently he went to get his jacket.

Marshall smiled. Jonathan had always been a sensitive boy, easily tuning into his mother's moods and needs. Side by side they strolled down the sidewalk. Lilacs were almost finished blooming, but

Marshall plucked a sprig off a bush they passed. She inhaled the sweet aroma of the purple blossoms, gathering up the courage to speak.

"So, what gives?" Jonathan asked when, after five minutes, Marshall had failed to say anything. "This is about him, right?"

"Him? Whom do you mean?" Marshall knew she was being deliberately obtuse, but needed to gain more time.

"You know who." The boy wasn't thrown off by her obvious tactics.

Marshall sighed. "Yes, it's about your father." She hesitated, not certain how he would react to what she was about to reveal. "I want to show you something."

They reached the park where Robert often had taken Jonathan to play. She knew he'd had no excuse to go there for years.

"Hey, this old park looks just the same as when Dad and I—" Jonathan stopped and kicked at a stone. "So, what did you want to show me? The cute baby swings?"

Marshall took a deep breath. "When your father began to drink heavily and became abusive, for too many years I simply put up with it. I'm sorry we didn't separate sooner because for your sake it would have been better. It's just that I always thought maybe there was something I could do to help him. Get him to stop drinking."

Jonathan gave her shoulder a pat. "Yeah, Mom. You've always been a fixer. And like a terrier you don't give up easily."

Marshall laughed. "I guess you're right." His understanding of her would make it easier to talk to him. "And although I finally saw that he wasn't going to stop—I still had a hard time giving up on him. I guess I didn't want to give up the dream we always had."

"What dream was that?"

"We planned that we would sell our house and sail around the world and visit all those little islands that are just tiny specks in the vast oceans. I would home school you and you'd be the most cosmopolitan, well-educated kid ever. And then, when our dance was over, your dad and I would totter down the hill together, hand in hand." A sob broke into her story. "My Jon Anderson and I." Her eyes misted. "That's the part I really had a hard time giving up on. I didn't want to even consider growing old without him."

"I see." Jonathan broke off a twig from a bush they passed and flipped it back and forth like a windshield wiper. "Sailing around the world would've been fun. Of course I would've missed my buddies." He grinned. "But I think it would've been a pretty cool way to live. Too bad it didn't happen."

"Yes. But here comes the part I'm sure you'll think is weird. Maybe difficult to understand."

"Try me." He flung the twig away, to signal he was ready to listen.

"When I finally was forced to concede that he wasn't going to change, I had to do something to convince myself that those dreams were never going to happen, and the man I'd married was gone . . . was as good as dead. And so I buried him."

Chapter Nine

Jonathan's steps came to an abrupt halt. "You buried him?"

"Yes."

They had arrived at an overgrown corner of the park where the grass was uncut and wild flowers grew undisturbed. Marshall pulled a few branches aside and exposed a tiny wooden plaque. It had Robert's name on it, written with indelible marker. She could hear Jonathan's quick, indrawn breath of disbelief. She couldn't blame him if he found this morbid. Even her friend, Kelly, who'd assured her she understood, had admitted later that her first reaction had been one of horror.

"Here's where I buried him," Marshall pressed on though she saw Jonathan take a step back. "I placed my favorite picture of him in a little blue velvet box. It's the one where he's smiling happily, without that sneer that became his trademark later on. I also put in some other items that reminded me of the way he used to be. And I buried them here."

"That's totally gruesome, Mom," Jonathan said with

a self-conscious snort. "Creepy."

Marshall was glad he didn't look at her as though she'd lost her marbles. Or worse, laugh at her.

"You know," Jonathan said, "I think I remember that blue velvet box. We came here together, didn't we?"

"Yes."

After a long silence he asked. "So, did it work?"

"I think so. When I told him it was over, I was able to be very firm and not waver in my determination, no matter what he said or did after that."

Only silence exists between them. She knows he won't leave until the house is sold.

"I've cooked too much spaghetti," she tells him one evening. "If you wish you may have some." She keeps her tone cold, matter-of-fact. Too late she realizes her mistake.

He eats with a relish, a big smile on his face. And after eating he is so helpful—loading the dishwasher, wiping the counter.

God help her! He is like a little boy. "See, I'm a good boy now, Mommy. You aren't angry with me any more, are you?" He thinks all is forgiven.

She has to steel herself to not look at him. Those little boy eyes rip open her heart.

Later, in her room she cries.

"It must have been hard for you, Mom."

"Yes, it was. But actually I didn't bring you here just to tell you about this. I wanted to ask you to do something, Jonathan."

"What?" There was a wary note in his voice.

"I thought maybe if you did the same thing . . ."

She could tell Jonathan was scowling even though she didn't look up at his six foot height.

"Same thing? Just what's that supposed to mean?"

Marshall knew he was ready to refuse whatever she was going to suggest. She hesitated, trying to make sure she phrased it in such a way that he wouldn't fling it back in her face.

"I thought maybe you could bury the father you hated, the one who didn't play with you, who always yelled at you no matter how hard you tried to please him. And then you could look differently at your new father."

Jonathan turned away and Marshall was afraid he would walk off. But he took only a couple of steps and stopped. He turned back to face her. "You're crazy, Mom."

"You think he didn't love you," she said earnestly. "But it was alcohol that made him treat you badly."

"Forget it, Mom. I'm not going to get chummy with an alcoholic. He can go on another bender at any time, so why go through all the hassle of reconnecting and then end up getting tossed aside again. I don't trust him. And neither should you."

"I realize that. And you may be right." Marshall's voice came out small and beaten.

"And yet you're willing to go through with this? I don't get it, Mom." He ran a hand through his hair. "You could be heading for heartbreak again."

"I know." Her voice now was merely a whisper. She hung her head, not wanting her son to see how he was crushing the hope she'd foolishly been building in her heart. "I know."

For a moment Jonathan was silent and then Marshall felt his hand gently stroke her hair.

"Sorry, but I'm not an undertaker, Mom. Not even for virtual burials."

"I just thought it might help."

"Yeah, it certainly would help *you*." Jonathan's voice turned ominously cold.

"What do you mean?" Though she knew exactly what he meant. "I'm only thinking it might help you if you—"

"Mom, I know what you're after. You want me to make peace with Dad so then you can have your cake and eat it too."

Although Marshall knew he was right, his accusing tone made her defensive. She made her voice sound shocked. "What exactly do you mean by that, Jonathan? That's not a nice thing to say to your mother."

He sighed. "Mom, you want us to be a cozy little family, just the way you always imagined we should have been, but never were. You want to get together with Dad, and if I just buried the hatchet, everything would be just peachy for you, wouldn't it? You'd have your man and your son, too."

"Yes," Marshall said defiantly. "I'd have the two men I love beyond anything in this world. But you don't want me to have that. Do you?"

Exasperated, Jonathan shook his fists in the air. "Mom, Mom! I want you to have everything you want in this life and you should know that. But don't expect me to jump through silly hoops like this burial thing. It's not going to happen. And I'm not going to get all buddy-buddy with Dad, not even to make you happy."

Marshall's lower lip quivered, and she turned to hide it from her son. "I'm sorry you thought this was silly. I was hoping you'd understand." She didn't want to make him feel guilty, but couldn't help sounding wounded. She was so utterly disappointed that her plan had failed.

"I understand why you felt you had to do it, Mom," Jonathan said. "And I'm glad it worked for you. But I don't want to do that. I decided long ago that he was out of my life, and I'd much rather keep it that way."

He turned and walked off toward the playground equipment. Marshall watched him go and the ache inside her almost squeezed the breath out of her. Because now she would have to give up Robert after just having found him again.

Jonathan walked past the swings and seemed bent on leaving the park. But when he got to the monkey bars he stopped. For a long while he just stood there. Then he reached up, took hold of the bars with both hands and did a couple of chin ups. Then, as Marshall watched, she saw him raise one hand to his face. Although his back was to her, she recognized the gesture. He was wiping away tears.

Marshall was about to follow her natural instinct and hurry to comfort her child, but common sense prevailed and she left him alone. It wouldn't have been fair to intrude on the man's private grief, not even to comfort him.

After a few moments he turned around to face his mother. He hung from the bars, pulling himself up so his feet were off the ground. To her relief, Marshall saw that he was smiling.

"Mom," he called. "Remember when Dad used to bring me here?"

"Of course I do." Slowly she walked over to him and he dropped to the ground.

"I remember the time when I was watching the big kids swing on these monkey bars and it looked like so much fun. I wanted to hang like that, too, and move my hands from one bar to the next, swinging like a monkey, but no matter how I kept jumping up I couldn't reach them. And then Dad lifted me up and I hung there like a sack of potatoes, trying to swing. I was scared as hell, but I gritted my teeth and hung on and with his support I was able to swing all the way across." There was a catch in his voice. When, after a long pause, he went on, his voice was husky. "I felt so big and brave."

Marshall reached up to touch his cheek.

At last Jonathan said quietly, "I'm lucky, I guess, to have been old enough so I can remember that. Olivia can't remember anything about him. Good or bad."

"And I'm sure if you let yourself remember, you'll find there were other good moments, too," Marshall said. "Things weren't always bad."

"Yeah, I know." Jonathan scratched at the chipped red paint on the metal bar. But his next words sent her world crashing down again. "But I don't trust him. I don't want to have him as my father ever again."

He couldn't hear the awful sound her heart made when it broke, because he casually wrapped his arm around her shoulders. "Let's go and watch a movie on TV, Mom. Some black & white silent pic from when you were a kid."

Marshall nodded. The huge lump in her throat prevented any sound from escaping.

Together they made their way back across the grassy playground, past the swings.

Suddenly Jonathan grabbed his mother by the waist. "Hey, Momsie, you wanna swing?" Without waiting for an answer, he picked Marshall up by the waist and, lifting her onto a black rubber seat, sent her flying. But her disappointed heart stayed on the ground, in the corner of the park where the wild flowers grew undisturbed.

"Do you want to stop somewhere for a bite?" Robert asked when he picked Marshall up from school.

She threw her books and purse in the back seat of his car. "I've got dinner cooking in the slow-cooker."

"How about stopping for a drink?" He turned the corner towards downtown.

"I have wine at home if I want some."

He seemed to like setting up these situations where he expected her to have alcohol. That annoyed her, although she knew they were his way of trying to show that she could trust him. Sometimes she took him up on his suggestion, but usually tried to avoid them.

"Robert," she began while he turned the car around and headed towards her home. She hesitated, but then decided to blurt it out. "Do you think you could ask Jonathan to come sailing with us sometime?"

Robert's laugh sounded far from humorous. "You've got to be kidding."

She had to try. "Maybe you two could make up for some of the lost father-son time."

"You know that won't happen. But, hey, if it means so much to you, then I guess I can at least try."

Marshall sighed with relief. "Thank you, Robert."

"After all," he went on, "it seems the only way you'll consent to have sex is if you're comfortable with this Jonathan thing."

His words hit her in the stomach like an iron fist.

"Robert!" Marshall yelped. "Is that the only thing that's important to you?"

"Well, no, but after our night in the hotel it's certainly up there among the top two on my list.

Second only to you."

"Forget about the night in the hotel. We agreed not to mention it. It was just a . . . a vacation from reality."

"Try telling that to my body. It aches for you every night so bad that—"

"Stop!" She was so angry she was beginning to tremble. Of course she experienced the same yearning for him, but they'd agreed not to talk about it.

"You're breaking your promise." She took a deep breath, trying to remain calm. "I thought I could trust you."

Robert looked down. "I'm sorry. You're right, of course. And I didn't mean to make a joke of it. That night was too precious to me. I apologize, Marshall." He reached over to touch her clenched hand on her lap.

She sat for a few moments, pursing her lips. "This is not what we were talking about."

"Oh yes. Jonathan."

She could hear the sneer. "How can you be so callous about this? If you'd seen the way he was moved by the memory of—" She stopped. She'd said too much.

"Memory of what?" Robert asked. "What was he moved about?"

Marshall hadn't meant to disclose the incident, but it was too late to turn back now, so she went on. "Of how big you made him feel when you held him up on the monkey bars at the park when he was little."

There was a long silence and then, "He was moved?"

"He was in tears. And you'd have been in tears, too, listening to him tell about it. But please don't say anything to him about that," Marshall pleaded. "I didn't mean to tell you. I know he wouldn't want you to know."

"Of course I won't say anything to him. We don't even talk to each other, so how could I say anything to him about anything?"

This kind of silly chatter had always been his way of covering up his emotions, when he didn't know what to do with them. Sometimes it had driven her wild.

"Don't make light of it. This is serious," she warned him.

"I know. I'm sorry. I just feel . . ." He ran a hand through his hair, a gesture that made her think of Jonathan. She hadn't realized how often Jonathan did that very same thing until she'd seen Robert do it.

"I guess I feel nervous," he conceded at last. "I don't want to screw this up, because if I do, I'll lose you."

Disappointment filled her. Didn't he care about regaining his son's love? "Is that the only reason?" she asked quietly.

"Marshall, you have to understand that *you* are the lode star toward which I'm striving with every fibre of my being. You. Not Jonathan. Not even Olivia. I'm sorry, but they're not as important to me at this point as you are. I don't really know them. I haven't missed them all these years like I've missed you. Do you understand, darling?"

Yes, she understood, but that didn't prevent her heart from being torn to pieces. She couldn't make him love his children. All she could do was try to survive the pain. The relationship between Robert and his children was beyond her. She had to stop trying to fix it.

She turned away from him so he wouldn't see the tears that flowed from her eyes. She didn't want to wipe them away because the gesture would have been a give-away. Instead she reached into her purse for a tissue and blew her nose, at the same time surreptitiously wiping her cheeks.

"I guess I understand," she said when she was sure her voice wouldn't wobble. "It's something you three are going to have to work out on your own." She could only cross her fingers and hope, and hope, and keep on hoping that one day the father and son would learn to love each other. Maybe tolerating each other was the best they could ever achieve, but that wasn't good enough for her. Marshall wanted more. She was greedy.

At least there was hope Robert would learn to love Olivia, who already adored him. She was like a puppy, giving of her love so freely and unconditionally, and naïvely expecting it to be returned in the same measure. Marshall feared Olivia was opening herself up to a lot of heartbreak in her life, being so open and trusting, but she also knew she was powerless to do anything about it. The thought did nothing to help stem her tears.

She had to stop trying to be a fixer.

The phone roused Robert from the half-sleep he'd fallen into while watching TV on the king bed in his hotel room.

It was the front desk. "A young lady is asking to come up to see you, sir. Shall I give her your room number?"

Robert sat up and rubbed his forehead sleepily. "A young lady?"

"She says she's your daughter, sir."

Olivia? Robert looked at the clock on the night table beside him. 11:45 p.m. What the hell . . .? "Please send her up."

Quickly he jumped into his jeans, which he'd already discarded earlier, pulled on his striped cotton shirt, and ran a hand through his hair.

Soon there was a faint knock on the door.

Olivia stood in the hall, looking slightly disheveled. And more than slightly drunk.

"Come in, Olivia," Robert said, after he'd recovered from the shock of seeing her like that.

The girl hobbled into the room on her high heels, trying to look dignified and sober. How well Robert remembered that feeling. He indicated the arm chair by the window and Olivia made her unsteady way over to it. She plunked herself down in a most undignified manner and kicked off her high heels. She looked tired, like she'd been walking for some time.

"So," Robert said in an attempt to start a conversation, but before he got any further, Olivia burst into tears.

"Don't be mad at me, Daddy!" she wailed. "I'm—hic —drunk!"

"I noticed," Robert said and then just waited. He didn't know where this was going, so he said nothing. It was probably the safest bet to let her lead.

"C'n I stay here with you? I can't go home like this! Mom would kill me. And she'd be so dis-appointed. And she would prob'ly cry. Please c'n I stay here with you?" This was punctuated with sobs and hic-cups.

Robert tried desperately to think of words that wouldn't jeopardize this whole thing. What should he do? What should he say in this situation? He reached into his brain for a bright idea, but came up empty-handed.

"But, Olivia, we can't let your mom sit at home and

worry," was the best he could think of.

"No. We—hic—can't."

"So I think we should give her a call and let her know you're safe. It's pretty late, you know. Do you often stay out this late?"

"How late?" She looked at him with huge, bleary eyes, the same blue as her mother's.

"Almost midnight."

Olivia burst into a fresh round of crying. "I never stay out this late!" she wailed. "I'm always home by 'leven, latest." She banged on the arm rest of the chair for emphasis. "Latest!"

"I believe you, Olivia. But now it's close to midnight so we better call—"

As if on cue the phone rang. It was Marshall. Her words came out in a panicky rush. "Robert, something has happened to Olivia. She hasn't come home. She's never been out this late without letting me know and—"

"Marshall, she's all right. She's right here with me."

"What? How come you didn't call and tell me?" Marshall's voice rose in anger to a high pitch and she went on, without giving him a chance to explain. "I've been worried out of my mind, ready to call the police, and here she's been having a pleasant evening with—"

"Darling," Robert was finally able to break into the stream. "She walked in not five minutes ago. We were just going to call you when you beat us to it."

"Oh."

"And after I've learned to what I owe this unexpected visit, I'll call you back. Okay? Bye, darling." And he hung up without giving Marshall a chance to agree or disagree.

Robert sat down on the edge of the bed, facing his daughter, who was still slumped in the chair, legs awry, her silky party skirt gathered up to her knees.

"So, where are you coming from?" Robert asked. He had no idea how a father would conduct this interview, but tried his best to sound firm yet friendly. That, he recalled from some magazine article, was the tone he was supposed aim for. Firm yet friendly.

"My friend's birth-hic-day party."

"Where was it?"

"At her house."

"Were her parents there?"

"I thought they were gonna to be there, an' I told Mom they were gonna to be there. But when I got there, they weren't there. I wasn' lyin' to her. Honest."

"I see. So it was just a bunch of kids, having a good time?"

"At first it was." Olivia looked at him with big, sincere eyes. "An' then it got rowdier 'n' rowdier an' they brought out beer 'n' stuff."

"What stuff?" He crossed his fingers. Please, not drugs.

"Pot 'n' stuff."

"So did you have any of this . . . this stuff?" Robert prayed the answer would be no.

Olivia looked down at her bare toes and wiggled them, obviously uncomfortable with the question. "Jus' some pot," she said in a small voice. Then she looked up at him with those big blue eyes that almost made him melt. "But, Daddy, I didn' have much."

Daddy. The word almost made him want to cry. For her to come here in her questionable condition, she obviously trusted him—her daddy.

"Have you done this sort of thing before, Olivia? Had alcohol and pot?"

She squirmed uncomfortably. "Just a tiny bit. I've

never been drunk or anythin'. Mom's really strict about me drinkin' al'cool. An' I haven't—'cept a coupla times, because mom is so strict about me drinkin' alcohol. Neurotic, almost. It's embarrassin'. Some of my friends drink, you know."

"Beer?"

"Yup."

"Has your mom ever told you why she's so strict?"

"Yeah. She's told me that some people can have a genetic dis-position to alcohol-ism and she's worried I could have it." Olivia raised her foot onto her knee and rubbed her big toe.

"She's right, you know," Robert said.

"Why would I have a genet—that thing? Mom drinks but she's not an alcoholic."

"I am."

Olivia's jaw dropped. "You are? I didn' know."

"Your mother never told you?"

"No." She sat, silent, for a few moments and Robert let the news sink in.

"Is that why you and mom got divorced?" she finally asked, almost in a whisper.

"Yes. Alcohol can do really bad things to a family relationship."

Olivia sat, chewing the end of a tendril of hair. He wanted to tell her to take it out of her mouth because it made him gag, but that would have distracted them from the issue.

"Gee, I wish I'd known," she said at last. "I wish Mom had trusted me an' told me. I'm not a baby any more, you know." She looked sullen.

"I'm sure she was going to tell you, eventually."

Annoyed, Olivia swung her leg. "Yeah, when? On her deathbed?"

Of course Robert didn't know Marshall's reasons for having withheld this information. And he wasn't sure he even agreed with her, but he had to try to defend her decision.

"Look, sweetheart, I'm sure she had it all figured out. She would have told you when she felt the time was right." Robert wanted to take this pouting girl in his arms, but didn't feel totally comfortable or ready to execute this fatherly gesture. How often should he have been there to comfort her, to advice her, to soothe her hurt, or calm her anger? And he wasn't. He wanted to cry from remorse and shame. Cry for the lost years and the lost opportunities to know his daughter and maybe even help her.

Olivia didn't reply. Robert saw that her eyelids were getting heavy and then he heard a soft snore coming from the depth of the armchair.

She was asleep.

He'd planned to drive her home but now changed his mind and instead carried her onto the bed and covered her with half of the king-sized duvet. He then called the front desk and asked for a cot to be brought into the room. He would have got himself another room, but he wanted to be close in case she woke up and was confused, or—more than likely—sick to her stomach.

Sick to her stomach! He called the desk again and asked for a basin and some wet wipes. Better be prepared.

Then he called Marshall and told her what was happening.

"I'll bring her home in the morning when she wakes up. And I think you should know I told her about my problem with alcohol."

"How did she take it?" Marshall asked. She didn't sound angry. Perhaps she was relieved this family secret was finally out in the open.

"Okay, I guess. But she's a bit pissed off with you for not telling her. Why didn't you?"

Marshall was silent for so long that he thought she'd also fallen asleep on him. "Marshall?" he asked.

"I . . . um . . . I didn't want to spoil her gilded image of her father," she said at last. "She's been so enamored with you all these years I didn't have the heart to tell her you were actually a big, drunken slob."

Robert wanted to laugh at her straightforward words but reprimanded her instead. "You could have expressed it some other way, you know. Something a bit more scientific or medical, for example."

"The last time I saw you, that's what you were," Marshall stated flatly. "A big, drunken slob. I didn't know you'd gone on a self-improvement program. As far as I knew you could still be living under a bridge somewhere."

"Okay, fair enough. Now go to bed, darling. I'll see you in the morning."

"Yes, I'm tired," Marshall said. "I've been so terribly worried all evening. Good night."

Robert sat looking at his sleeping daughter. Marshall hadn't wanted to spoil Olivia's . . . how had she put it? Gilded image of him. God, how could he live up to such a picture of perfection? Having now reappeared in her life, he hoped he wouldn't come crashing down.

A soft knock on the door told him the cot and basin had arrived.

Chapter Ten

Robert didn't sleep well, listening to Olivia's raspy, drunken breathing. That's what Marshall had gone through with him, only a hundred times worse. Remorse filled him. He didn't deserve to have the love of these two wonderful women. What had made him think he could just waltz into these people's lives? Utter selfishness!

The sight of Marshall at the funeral had filled him with such longing that it had blinded him to every other consideration. He wanted her back, but hadn't thought about how this would affect her life. Or Olivia's life. Or, God help him, Jonathan's life.

Well, the boy—the man—his son—wasn't having any part of him, and Robert was okay with that. No, he wasn't. But he understood. He didn't deserve for the boy to acknowledge him as his father. Much less to love him.

Love! What did he know about loving his kids? Marshall he loved with all his heart, but Olivia? She was already on the brink of womanhood, and he'd missed all the childhood experiences. The diapers, the first steps, the first words, first tooth, all the firsts and the thousands of days after that. And there was no way to rewind and play again those missed times. Why did life have to be so unfair? You got one kick at the can, and if you screwed up, that was it. And, boy, had he ever screwed up!

Robert sat up and reached for the remote. Might as well watch TV. At least that would take his mind off these thoughts.

Just then Olivia whimpered in her sleep, alerting him to a possible emergency.

Yes! She raised her head and made a sound that made him grab the basin and quickly bring it directly under her chin.

When she'd finished vomiting, he wiped her lips and helped her up so she could go and rinse her mouth in the bathroom.

"There's an unused toothbrush still in the package, if you want to brush your teeth," he called to her. "It should be there, on the counter."

At last, looking like a bedraggled kitten, she came from the bathroom and sat on the edge of the bed. "My head hurts," she whimpered.

"That's called a hangover," Robert said, and did his best not to sound sympathetic. Might as well have her suffer the pangs and arrows of having guzzled too much booze.

"Is there something you can give me for it?" she appealed.

"Sorry. I don't have anything." He did, of course, but wasn't about to alleviate her pain in any way. "Best go back to sleep. I'll drive you home in the morning."

Olivia hung her head. "Mom will kill me," she said morosely.

Robert wanted to laugh, but kept his face serious. "No she won't. I'll be there to protect you," he said. "Now go to sleep."

And once again the room was silent, save for the deep, uneven breathing of his daughter. His drunk daughter.

Robert turned on the TV and put the volume on mute.

"Where's Olivia?" Robert asked, and hung his light jacket in the hall closet. No longer feeling like a visitor, he didn't even knock before entering. He was family. And Marshall was happy with that.

"She's spending the evening at her friend's. They're working on a project together."

Robert raised a questioning eyebrow. "Are you sure about that?"

"Of course I'm sure. Emma's a good girl." She paused. "Just like Olivia."

"You trust Olivia? After what she did?"

"Of course I trust her. Just because a kid messes up once you don't stop trusting her."

As soon as she'd said that, she knew what would follow.

"And how about me? How's your trust level with me?"

Marshall sighed with exasperation. "Robert, when you ask things like that you're just cruisin' for a bruisin'." She went into the kitchen and came out with a glass of wine, which she carried into the family room. "Get yourself a soft drink if you want. There's some in the fridge." She hoped he wouldn't continue on the topic.

Robert got his soda and followed her into the family

room. "I screwed up once, and that means I'm out for the count?"

Marshall burst out into an incredulous laughter. "My God, Robert! Think what you just said. You screwed up more than once. More like a hundred times. Ten hundred times!"

"So you're saying a thousand?"

"Oh, stop splitting hairs!" Marshall snapped. "But I'm sure it's not that far off the mark."

"You keep dredging up the past," Robert exploded. "You don't seem to appreciate that I'm doing my best to stay sober."

"You brought it up, not me." Marshall saw that the situation was in danger of escalating into one of those ludicrous arguments they'd always had in the past. It started from nothing, and the next thing she knew they were in the middle of a heated fight, dredging up all the silly nonsense from the past. Sometimes they even brought their families into the foray, fighting about whose father or mother had done what at which Thanksgiving or Christmas dinner.

And after it was all over, they had always made up by having great sex.

The arguing was something Marshall had definitely not missed in all these years without Robert. And here they were at it again.

"Robert," Marshall said and sat down beside him. As if on cue his arm went around her and he pulled her close. But she disengaged herself from it and firmly placed his hand on his knee. "Robert, do you see what we're doing just now?"

"Sitting on the couch?"

"Stop being silly. You know what I mean."

"Okay. Arguing?"

"Yes, and did you notice how it started?"

He was silent, thinking back. "I asked where Olivia was."

"Yes, and then it became about me trusting her. And about me not trusting you, and how many times you screwed up and all that sort of nonsense, until we were almost at each other's throats."

Robert was silent again. "I see. And so you didn't want me to put my arm around you so we wouldn't end this by kissing and having sex?"

"Yes. See how easy it would have been to slide back into the old way of settling things?"

"I guess old habits die hard."

Marshall faced him and looked him square in the eye. "There's one thing I want you to understand, Robert. You say I don't appreciate that you are trying to stay sober. Well, I do appreciate it and I'm very glad for you. But guess what? It's your circus, my dear and they're your monkeys. You want to stay sober? That's fabulous. But whether you succeed or not, is not up to me. Remember that."

She didn't add that she couldn't help hoping with all her heart that he would succeed. Or that if he failed she would probably die.

They sat silently for a long time. Marshall sipped her wine, hoping he wouldn't see that her hand was unsteady. She still couldn't help feeling like a heel drinking in front of him. She had to get over that. He'd told her he wanted her to be at ease about it, but it was more difficult than she could ever have imagined.

"So, can I touch you now that we're not arguing any more?" Robert finally asked. "It's very difficult to sit here bedside you and not have my arm around you. It just doesn't seem natural."

Marshall laughed. "I would like it very much if you put your arm around me. But first let me turn on the TV. If Olivia walks in and we're just sitting here cuddling in the dark—"

"She would probably be really happy." His arm went around her shoulders. "She wants us to get together, you know. And I'm sure she knows why we didn't come home after the party."

Marshall reached for the converter and clicked the On button. The TV screen lit up but she had no idea what program came on, because Robert had pulled her close and was kissing her.

She wrapped her arms around his neck and her heart raced as their kiss deepened. This was not because they'd been arguing, she told herself. They had talked about it afterwards instead of jumping into bed to make love.

God, how she wanted him to undress her and carry her into the bedroom. She needed to have him there, between her legs. She needed to feel the weight of his body on her. She needed—

The door slammed and they jumped apart like guilty teenagers.

"Hello, I'm home!" Olivia sang out. "Hi, Daddy! Hi, Mom!"

"Greeted you first, I noticed," Marshall whispered. But she felt happy about it. That relationship seemed to be blossoming.

"She's just being polite to a visitor," Robert whispered back and then called, "Hi, Olivia! I'm glad you came home before I left."

"Why do you always have to go back to the hotel? Why don't you stay here for the night some time?" Olivia asked, coming into the room. She dumped her bag of books on the coffee table with a thunk. "Emma and I got a lot of work done tonight. You want to see what we were working on, Daddy?"

"I sure would," Robert enthused and Olivia pulled her books out to show him.

"I'll go and make us some tea," Marshall said. Her heart sang as she went into the kitchen. Maybe with Jonathan the relationship wasn't proceeding as well as she would have hoped—in fact, it wasn't proceeding at all—but with Robert and Olivia things were sailing along smoothly.

"I think our daughter is going to be a scientist," Robert said after he and Olivia had gone over her project. "Or maybe an environmentalist. She has some really neat ideas for constructing a hydroponic garden."

Olivia blushed with pleasure. "It would be great if you could help me with this some time," she said. "Maybe some evening next week? You could give me hints on how to build the structure."

"That would be fine, as long as it's okay with your mother." He sent a questioning look at Marshall.

She nodded. "I don't see why not."

Yes, then he would have a very good excuse to be here more often. But after the way she'd just responded to his kisses, she didn't know how far she could trust herself.

"I'm really looking forward to us all going sailing this weekend," Olivia said as she packed away her papers. "I just wish Jonathan could make it, too."

"You and Emma will have a great time rowing in the dinghy," Marshall said. "But, yes, it would nice if Jonathan could come. Young men are just so busy with their own lives . . ." But she knew this young man wouldn't have come even if he had nothing else to do.

"But you and Emma be careful on the highway when you drive up," Robert said, frowning. "Are you sure Emma's a competent driver? How long has she had her license?"

"She just got her permanent, but she's always very careful," Olivia told him. "Don't worry, Daddy. She's good."

This show of parental concern, a side of Robert that she hadn't seen before, made Marshall's heart sing.

As she was seeing Robert off at the door, he put his arms around her and whispered, "I like Olivia's suggestion that I stay over some night." His smiled mischievously and her heart went into overdrive. "Don't you think that's a good idea?"

Marshall tried to push him away with both hands. "No, I definitely do *not* think it's a good idea."

He held her tightly against him. "We have a very smart daughter," he said loudly enough for Olivia to hear in the family room. He kissed Marshall good-night.

Standing at the open door she watched him walk down to where his Corvette was parked on the driveway. In the glow of the porch light she saw his hair blowing in the brisk spring breeze. He turned and waved to her with a broad grin that had never failed to excite her, ever since she'd first seen it way back in high school.

Overnight? God, what would happen if he stayed? They couldn't very well have another "just pretend" night. It would mean that she was committing herself to getting back together with him. Marshall could tell that her barricades were in danger of starting to crumble.

And if it weren't for Jonathan, she was sure they would already have fallen.

Robert and Marshall drove up to the boat Friday evening right after school with a carload of food. Olivia and Emma would follow later, after Emma had finished her after-school shift at the local coffee shop. They would all spend the night on the boat in order to get an early start the following morning. Their destination the next day was Club Island, a small half-moon shaped island in the bay.

"There are some dilapidated log cabins left over from the time when the island had some gravel industry or other," Robert had told Olivia. "Now there's just the wharf and some rusted cables, and mounds of gravel to tell the story. I think you and Emma will like exploring it."

Robert and Marshall entered through the marina gates. Soon the sun would set, so they stuffed the food inside the boat and then quickly closed the slides.

Marshall slapped at a mosquito on her arm. "These infamous Georgian Bay mosquitoes haven't changed their habits. They still attack at sunset."

After organizing all the things they had brought with them, they sat in the cabin, softly illuminated by an oil lamp and waited for the girls to arrive. The boat swayed gently whenever one of them moved.

"The 'halyard orchestra' is quiet tonight," Robert remarked.

"Yes, it's nice and peaceful, isn't it," Marshall agreed. "I remember how the clanging of halyards against the masts used to keep me awake on windy nights."

Although other boat owners had also come to spend the night, the closed slides kept out all intruding sounds. The quiet intimacy in the cabin was pleasant, but Marshall wished the girls would arrive soon.

Memories of nights spent making love in their old boat came flooding back, and desire built up inside her. Could she trust herself if Robert started to make amorous moves?

As if reading her thoughts, Robert laughed. "You look very uncomfortable, honey. That doesn't say much for your trust in me."

"It's not that," she protested, "I just hope nothing's happened on the highway."

"Oh, Marsha, Marsha, who're you trying to kid? You're worried I might start to—" He rose slightly as if to move over to her side of the cabin.

"Robert, please stay where you are," Marshall said with a slight laugh, hoping that hid the desperation in her voice.

"Why? Are you afraid the boat will tip over if we're both on the same side?"

"Don't be silly. I know it won't."

With a sudden move Robert shifted over to sit beside her. Just as quickly he brought her around to face him.

"This is what you're afraid of." And his mouth came down hard on hers, leaving her gasping for air. Then, just as suddenly he let her go and moved back to his side of the cabin. He sat there with an irritatingly satisfied grin on his face.

Marshall wiped her mouth and frowned with pretend anger. "You still get such a kick out of teasing me, don't you? You're nothing but a big silly kid!" But she couldn't deny she loved that side of him. She'd missed the teasing. And, of course, the kisses.

Robert winked mischievously. "And you love it, don't you?"

"I do not!" Marshall said vehemently. And then, in

an effort to compose herself, she changed the subject. "I sure hope this trip won't be too uncomfortable with four people on board. It would be a shame to spoil a nice sail, having a couple of teen-agers along who can't find anything to do, away from their iPods."

"You invited them."

"I know. But I hope it wasn't a mistake."

"Face it, sweetheart, you just didn't want to spend the night alone with me." But Robert's voice was congenial and relaxed and gradually the tension left her.

"I still think it's too bad Jonathan couldn't come," she said. "You did ask him, didn't you?"

"I told you I did. And I was lucky I was on the phone or I'm sure the kid would've spat in my face." His laugh was humorless.

Marshall wanted to cry. She shouldn't have even suggested the invitation. It had put Robert in a very unpleasant position, being verbally slapped in the face by his son. He had called Jonathan just to please her, and to show he was making an effort.

Just then the boat rocked with heavy footsteps as people clambered on board. "Let us in before these mosquitoes suck us dry!" Olivia cried and added to the pandemonium by pounding impatiently on the roof.

Robert was already up, removing the slides, and the two people slid down the steps with their luggage, accompanied by dozens of whining mosquitoes. One of the two was not Emma. Marshall stared, open mouthed, while Robert quickly shut the slides and turned around to stare at Jonathan.

"Jonathan!" Marshall stammered, "What are you doing here?"

"Emma wasn't feeling well, so Olivia begged me to

come, with tears flowing down her face." Jonathan looked slightly uncomfortable, but then he smiled wryly. "Aren't you glad to see me?" He bent over and gave Marshall a kiss on the cheek, but failed to greet his father. His large frame and Olivia's smaller one filled the cabin.

"I suggest we all sit down," came Robert's cool voice and at his words everyone found a place on the berths. Jonathan seated himself beside Marshall.

Robert stuffed their duffel bags out of the way into the bow, and sat down beside Olivia. His face was stony, giving a good indication of how he felt about this new development.

"I believe introductions are in order," chirped Olivia. "Daddy, this is Jonathan. Jonathan, this is Daddy."

Jonathan scowled. "Don't be silly, Olivia."

Olivia pouted at her brother. "I want to be silly. You were such a grouch all the way here that I need to be silly! If you didn't want to come, why did you agree? I don't want to have you around all grumpy the whole weekend."

"I agreed because you were hysterical at the thought of not being able to go sailing," Jonathan riposted. "Like that would have been the end of the world."

"Everything will be all right," Marshall said calmly and patted her son's knee beside her. If only she could believe that herself.

For a while everyone was silent, as if waiting for the other shoe to drop.

At last Jonathan had to look at Robert, who sat right in front of him. "Nice boat," he said stiffly.

"Thanks," Robert replied with steel in his voice.

"I think it's really cute!" Olivia commented and took in the whole cabin with one turn of her head.

"Which means you think it's very small, right?" Robert said with a smile.

"No. I think it's very cozy," Olivia said "Like compact."

"Small," Robert pronounced.

"Isn't anyone going to offer me a nightcap?" Jonathan broke in.

Marshall frowned. Jonathan was obviously doing it again—playing up his drinking in front of his father. It almost seemed like he deliberately wanted to get under Robert's skin. As soon as they were alone, Marshall decided, she would confront him and demand he put a stop to this charade. Of course in the confines of the small vessel, having a private conversation would be difficult, if not impossible.

She got up, picked a bottle from the wine rack and dug a beer for Jonathan from a cooler. "Get your father and yourself a soft drink, Olivia," she said. They're in that little fridge."

As the evening wore on, Olivia kept up a stream of chatter and didn't seem to mind that she got only sparse responses. Jonathan and Robert faced each other, making no further overtures while Marshall squirmed uncomfortably.

She was relieved when at last Robert looked at his watch and said, "In order to get an early start tomorrow morning, I suggest we hit the sack." It was a command, not a suggestion, and everyone rose at once, ending up standing nose to nose in the narrow cabin. No one was able to budge.

"The ladies will sleep in the bow," Robert said. "It's more private there. Jonathan, you can sit down until they have removed themselves from this area." Again it was an order, not a request, and Jonathan complied with a shrug.

With a maximum of commotion everyone found a place to sleep and they were finally settled down for the night.

But in the morning the pandemonium was repeated, until everyone had eaten breakfast and found a place somewhere on the boat, either in the cockpit or up on the deck.

The twenty-mile voyage to Club Island took most of the day. Marshall missed the friendly camaraderie of the previous trip with Robert and she was annoyed with Olivia for having forced Jonathan to come along. Now she would be uptight all weekend, trying to make everyone's life as pleasant as possible, and it would be a tense two days for both Robert and Jonathan. Only Olivia—oblivious to the strain on board—would be able to enjoy the sail.

Robert was uncommunicative, busying himself with the sails and the tiller. He didn't ask anyone for help, and made the others feel incompetent and useless while he scampered on deck to tug at this pulley or pull at that sheet, and then hurried back to straighten the roaming tiller. Except for getting the meals and snacks, there was nothing for the rest of them to do.

Their progress was slow in the light breeze and, with the sun beaming down on the little boat, they soon stripped down to bare essentials. In her bikini, Marshall climbed up on the deck and joined Olivia, who was lying at the bow on a large beach towel in her bathing suit.

Robert sat on the coaming, one foot lazily working the tiller while gripping the back stay with one hand. Marshall tried not to look, but found it difficult to keep her eyes from straying toward him. Despite being middle aged, he was still muscular and narrow-hipped. The sight of his glistening broad shoulders awakened in her a yearning to slide her hands along his skin and feel the hard muscles. His piercing eyes were directed toward the horizon, as if he were deliberately ignoring the irritating presence of everyone else on board.

Jonathan came up to join Marshall and Olivia on the deck and sat, leaning his back against the aluminum mast. When he spoke his voice carried to every corner of the boat and it was obvious the words were meant to annoy Robert.

"It sure is good to just relax on a day like this, instead of hopping around the boat. But to each his own, I guess."

Robert obviously chose to ignore the comment and continued his silence. Not even Olivia's funny comments could draw a spirited response from him. Marshall knew he was furious because the weekend sail they'd been looking forward to was now spoiled by Jonathan's presence. Here she'd been worried about two teenage girls feeling bored, and instead she now had to contend with a much bigger problem.

They arrived at Club Island harbour in the late afternoon. Again, Robert didn't ask for any help as he lowered the sails and got the anchor ready. Jonathan had always been eager to lower the anchor and Marshall was sure Robert remembered that.

She was furious with the two men who were doing their best to deliberately make things as unpleasant as possible. Didn't they see or care how this was affecting her? It took all her willpower to not stand on the deck and scream at them. Or, better still, push them both overboard to cool off.

After supper Olivia asked Jonathan to go rowing with her around the basin. "I want to pick some of those pretty water lilies," she said.

Jonathan yawned. "I'm too lazy. Why don't you ask your father."

"Daddy has done all the work of sailing today," Olivia persisted. "I think he has a right to relax. And the exercise will do you good, big fat bro."

Reluctantly, Jonathan rose.

"Well, it's his fault if he's tired," Marshall heard him mutter as he helped Olivia get down into the dinghy. "He could've asked for help."

She watched as Jonathan began to row toward the shore. "He still knows how to row," she said to Robert. "Remember how good he was?"

As the dinghy drew farther away from the sloop, Marshall came down into the cockpit. Although the evening was warm, she'd pulled on a loose jersey top and pants over her swimsuit. Robert was still in his shorts.

It was time to confront the captain.

"Robert, I think you're being obnoxious," Marshall began bluntly. "You are being extremely cold toward Jonathan and your grumpiness is spoiling things for everyone. Especially me."

Robert didn't reply at once. When finally he turned to look at her, his eyes were cold. "I don't suppose it has occurred to you that I would rather have spent this weekend in the company of people I like, rather than with him." He waved his hand dismissively toward the dinghy that was slowly making its way along the shoreline.

Marshall bit her lip and lowered her head to stop

herself from lashing out angrily at him. "I'm sorry you don't want Jonathan along," she said. "But he's here and it wouldn't hurt if you showed him some common courtesy."

"Well, I haven't seen him showing me any courtesy," Robert persisted. "Common or otherwise."

These words had the effect of freeing Marshall's tongue.

"How childish can you be, a grown man!" she cried. "You sound like some of my pupils. Do you really think that two wrongs will make a right? As an older adult, couldn't you try to be friendly, despite his sullen reactions? How do you think things will ever get better if you and he both keep glowering at each other like two bulls?"

Robert took a careful sip of his soft drink and swallowed before speaking. His tone was quieter and no longer quarrelsome. "You're right, you know. I've been a lousy host, but unfortunately I can't promise that I'll be any more friendly where he is concerned. That may be beyond my powers. But I have no right to make the weekend miserable for you and Olivia." He smiled wryly. "I'm sorry I've been grumpy."

Marshall reached over and impulsively put a conciliatory hand on his arm. "We still have tomorrow."

Robert covered her hand with his. Their eyes met and held. Without a word she heard him tell her how much he loved and wanted her. But then he patted her hand, dissolving the moment with his mischievous grin.

"But if you keep running around in that bikini of yours, I don't know what will happen. I forcefully remind you that I find your near-naked body very enticing."

Marshall felt the heat rise to her face, partly from his words, partly from remembering her own thoughts when she'd ravished his muscular chest with her eyes.

Robert obviously saw her discomfort because he hastened to add, "But you needn't worry. There's hardly enough room here to move around, never mind finding a quiet corner for stolen kisses. Or anything more intimate, for that matter."

With the sun getting lower and lower, Olivia and Jonathan returned. He was rowing furiously to get them inside the boat before the hoards of mosquitoes attacked.

Once they were all safely in the cabin, Olivia glowed with enthusiasm. "We're going out at the crack of dawn to catch some of those whoppers we saw jumping in the bay," she said eagerly.

Jonathan joined in, and for the first time on the trip he sounded alive. "Olivia had me stop on the highway to buy some worms. I didn't really think we'd be needing them, but let me tell you, if it weren't for the blasted mosquitoes we'd be out there right now catching us some breakfast."

"Too bad we can't fit more than two in the dinghy," Olivia said. "You two would probably like to come along."

Marshall shook her head.

"No thanks," Robert said. "I'm not much into fishing. But you two go ahead and do your stuff."

Olivia and Jonathan spent the rest of the evening hunting for fishing gear in every nook and cranny of the boat.

Chapter Eleven

The next morning, just as the sun peeked over the horizon, the two fishermen got down into the dinghy with a clatter of fishing gear and banging of oars against the hull. At last they pushed themselves free of the sailboat.

Out of a porthole in the bow Marshall watched the pair row off. She laughed. "They tried to move so quietly so we wouldn't be disturbed."

She and Robert were both wide awake by now. He got up to make coffee, but she didn't want to leave the warmth and comfort of her sleeping bag.

"Get up, you lazy woman," Robert called at last. "The sun is up and the coffee is ready and we are going for a refreshing morning swim."

Marshall yawned. "Correction. *You* are going for a refreshing morning swim. I'll just crawl out to soak up some morning sun while I drink my coffee."

"Coward."

She heard him up on deck and soon the boat was rocked by the recoil of his dive. Marshall wiggled out of her sleeping bag and quickly slipped a light cotton dress over her panties. She emerged into the cockpit, coffee mug in hand, and watched Robert splash about like a young dolphin. He was naked, his limbs clearly visible though the pellucid water.

"Come on in!" he called to her. "It so invigorating! You'll love it!"

"It's too cold," Marshall protested, hugging herself. But she was beginning to regret her decision. The crystal clear water looked very inviting.

"Not once you're in, it's not. Come on!" Robert coaxed.

All at once Marshall laid down the mug and, without giving herself a chance to reconsider, climbed over the life lines and leaped into the water. The coldness hit her like a giant ice cube and she shrieked in shock.

"Liar!" she yelled. "You dastardly villain! This water is freezing!"

Her dress billowed up around her and she knew her bare legs and panties were clearly visible through the clear water.

Of course this fact drew Robert close to her. Treading water, he reached over to take her by the waist.

"Wow! Look at this lovely mermaid that just plopped down to play with me!" He wiggled his eyebrows lecherously and his hands caressed her hips and then slid down to her crotch. "Hey, whaddya know, she doesn't even have a fishtail. I'll be darned if she doesn't have a nice slit right here, between her two legs. How convenient!"

He quickly slid his naked torso between her legs and Marshall felt his firm, hard belly against her thighs. His hardness pressed against her crotch and she had a mad urge to claps him against her with her legs. Instead she pushed him away. "You let me go this instant!" she scolded him. "I mean it. I'm freezing."

"Killjoy." Reluctantly he released her.

Marshall swam back to the boat, but to her consternation she discovered she had no way of climbing back on board.

"How do I get up?" she wailed with a touch of panic in her voice. "There's no dinghy."

"It's easy," Robert said and swam to the stern. He grabbed hold of the coaming and, using the rudder as a step, easily pulled himself up. "Just like that."

Marshall tried to follow his example, but found that her arms weren't strong enough to pull up her weight.

"Help me, Robert!" she begged, "I can't do it." Exhausted, she fell back into the water. "Hurry, before I turn into an ice cube."

Robert reached down and gripped her outstretched arm. He pulled at her while she clutched a stanchion post with the other hand, hindering the process by laughing hysterically. Finally she managed to make an ungraceful entry into the cockpit and lay on the seat in a giggling, shivering heap.

Unceremoniously Robert threw a towel on top of her. "There. That's for not wanting to play with me," he said. "And you call yourself a primary teacher."

Marshall stood up and began to dry her hair vigorously. "But you're no primary child."

Which was the wrong thing to say. She felt Robert's intense eyes on her. "No, I'm not," he quipped. "I'm really glad you noticed."

Her arms froze and she became aware of how Robert was staring at her breasts with desire. Her nipples were taut with cold, and very visible through her wet dress. Quickly she brought the towel down to cover herself, but it was too late.

"You're the very picture of seduction," Robert said huskily. "There's nothing left to imagination. I see every lovely, desirable contour of your body."

Marshall shivered, but this time it wasn't from the cold. The dark fire in his eyes made her quiver with anticipation and desire.

"Darling, please," he pleaded.

The longing in his voice wrung her heart, and she yearned to touch him. The towel dropped as her arms went out to receive him. Only a step, and he held her, crushing his mouth against hers. Her hands caressed his broad, naked shoulders as they had wanted to do since long ago yesterday. She slid her palms down his back, absorbed by the sweet, wet sensation of the smooth rippling muscles under her palms. She was only half aware of his hands, drawing the shoulder straps down to bare her breasts. She clutched his naked buttocks and pressed them against her, wanting to feel his erection against her. Wanting it inside her.

They clung to each other like drowning people and his lips sought her neck, shoulders, breasts, until they once more found her mouth. She was gloriously conscious of her body throbbing to life under his ardent caresses.

He gathered up the hem of her dress and peeled the wet panties down her legs. As their bodies slid down onto the seat, Marshall looked up into his eyes, and found them hazy with love. Sighing deeply she opened herself to him and yielded to the fires inside her that demanded complete surrender.

Without waiting, Robert slipped inside her, filling her so completely that she could only moan with the indescribable pleasure of it all.

"Yo-hoo! We're back!"

The shout pierced through the mist of ecstasy that engulfed her brain and her eyes snapped open in panic. Marshall gave a soft whimper of disappointment as Robert drew himself out of her with a groan.

"Damn their timing," he cursed, as he shot down into the cabin.

"Anybody home?" Olivia's voice rang clearly over the water, although they were still at a distance.

Marshall found her panties, but couldn't pull the wet fabric up her legs quickly enough. She abandoned the effort and instead balled them up in her hands and threw them through the companionway into the cabin where Robert grabbed them and hid them under a seat cushion.

Marshall smoothed down her dress and pulled up the shoulder straps, while Robert, having tugged on his bathing trunks, climbed back into the cockpit to welcome the fishermen. He waved a casual greeting to the approaching pair and dove into the cool waters to calm down his body. Any telltale signs of her own desire were hidden by the damp dress.

With strong strokes Robert swam toward the fishermen.

Olivia brandished two good-sized bass. "Lunch!" she cried triumphantly, while Jonathan attached the dinghy to the stern.

"What are you doing back so soon?" Robert asked, taking a hold of the dinghy and floating casually behind it.

"Olivia managed to tip the can of bait overboard," Jonathan replied, forgetting to be surly.

But by the time they were on board he had again

resumed his sullen mask. Olivia, on the other hand launched into a detailed explanation of who had caught which fish and how it had all played out.

The day passed pleasantly enough, although, to Marshall's chagrin, whenever Jonathan spoke he didn't include his father in the conversation. She was uncomfortably aware of how Robert's eyes narrowed and his jaw clenched in anger. Although there wasn't much room, the two men were able to avoid contact, with Robert reading in the cockpit and Jonathan mostly lying down at the bow. Throughout the morning the two spoke no more than a couple of words to each other.

After lunch they all went to explore the island. Robert ferried them over in the tiny dinghy one at a time and they spent a few hours inspecting the ruins of the gravel operation and peeking into the dilapidated log cabins that had housed the island residents. Most of the roofs had caved in and the floorboards were rotten, but something of the inhabitants remained. Growing wild on the rocky earth were clumps of forget-me-nots and lilies of the valley. And among the trees that had invaded the clearings that had once been yards, there grew gnarled bushes of purple lilacs, all telling of a feminine presence. The only animals they saw were rabbits, which had multiplied freely in their island paradise. They were almost tame and seemed to have no fear of the visitors.

The remnants of this once flourishing settlement reminded Marshall of her own marriage that had once been so happy and thriving, but had fallen to ruin. She knew this community would never be resurrected, but what about her relationship with Robert? She hoped their visit to this crumbling community didn't bode ill for her own future happiness.

After dinner it was time to begin the preparations for their departure. Marshall was looking forward to the night sail, so she could show Olivia a different side of cruising. The lights from all the buoys, and on the distant shores, would flash red, yellow or green, in a dizzying array of long and short blinks. One would send three short, red blinks, while another might show two yellow flashes followed by a longer one. She liked to find them on the navigation map that Robert kept on the seat in the cockpit, and she hoped Jonathan would show interest in this, as he had, years ago.

She and Jonathan had loved to look up at the vast night sky with no city lights to dim the stars. Using binoculars they had discovered even more stars, and she was sure he still remembered all this. But tonight, would he even allow himself to take part in this activity?

Robert listened to the weather forecast. "We might be in for a spectacular display of lightning instead of a starry night," he said. "There's the threat of a thunder storm, with possible high winds and rain. It's from all that hot weather we've been having the last few days." He hoped it wouldn't be as fierce as the forecast had warned.

Olivia and Marshall filled thermos jugs with hot soup and coffee and made sandwiches to eat during the sail.

"We should be at Wingfield Basin sometime after midnight," Robert said. "It's a nice, quiet harbour where we can anchor and sleep until morning. Then, after breakfast we'll continue on to the marina."

"Sounds like a plan," Olivia said eagerly and screwed on the top of a thermos.

By nightfall they had left Club Island well behind and were heading south toward the mainland. The setting sun was soon obliterated by a great bank of dark clouds that rose across the horizon. As the cloud advanced, the lake was whipped white by the strengthening wind.

Darkness fell and the flashes of lightning in the distance became more and more visible. When they were followed by deep rumblings, Robert automatically counted the intervals—one thousand, two thousand, three thousand—as he'd done since he was a kid. But the storm was still far in the distance.

They donned their heavy sweaters, boots, oilskins and life jackets, for the waves were now breaking over the bow with increasing frequency, sending showers of spray into the cockpit. Robert had reefed the mainsail twice and the storm jib was ready to replace the working jib. A swaying storm lantern, attached to one of the backstays, was like a firefly fluttering in a bottle, throwing a spot of light into the darkness.

As the night wore on, the storm strengthened and Robert saw by the faces of his crew that they were getting apprehensive. Especially Olivia, who had never been sailing before. He tried to lift the serious mood by making light of the situation. There was, after all, nothing threatening them except possibly the discomfort of getting wet.

"Somehow I had visions of a different sort of experience," Olivia commented miserably, huddling like a yellow gnome in the corner of the cockpit, her face pinched by the cold wind and spray.

"And what is wrong with this?" Robert quipped. "I arranged it all especially for you so you'd have something exciting to tell Emma. Make her jealous for having missed it all."

"Thanks, Dad, but I was kinda expecting something more along the lines of a starry night and a full moon," Olivia muttered from her corner.

Robert laughed. "I'll arrange that for you next time." He hoped she was getting accustomed to the movement of the tossing yacht and wouldn't be too nervous.

But getting too complacent wasn't a good thing, either.

"I have to warn you about becoming too inattentive and careless as you get used to the movement of the boat," he warned. "The old sailors have a saying, 'One hand for yourself and one hand for the ship'. Remember that when you get up and move about."

Olivia—and even Jonathan—nodded, their faces serious.

"Although," Robert continued reassuringly, "it seems that in heavy weather most people are always more cautious than normal. So the danger of falling overboard is greater in good weather, when you might get a bit too complacent."

He saw Marshall shudder as she looked out at the dark heaving seas. "I'd hate to take a swim out there now," she said.

"Not as nice as this morning, that's for sure," Robert agreed. Falling overboard at night was no joke. Finding a person among waves this size would be impossible, even during the day.

Olivia turned her back on a wave that had warned of its approach with an ominous hiss. It sprayed them and then withdrew for a new attack.

"How big do you think the waves are now, Daddy?" she asked.

"It's hard to tell. But being a modest fellow I like to underestimate the size. Maybe two or three metres. But you know we sailors like to brag like fishermen, so you can easily chop off a foot or so from any wave you hear about."

Robert was relieved to hear everyone laugh at this, and little by little the mood in the cockpit changed from fearful apprehension to one of cautious enjoyment of the exciting experience.

"Hey, Marshall," Robert called out over the sound of the storm. "How about some hot coffee and sandwiches for everyone."

There was another flash of lightning, followed immediately by the clap of thunder directly overhead. A squall made the yacht heel over, making everyone grab for something to hold.

"You stay seated, Mom," Jonathan said. "I'll get the food."

He went down, stepping over the bottom slide that was in place to prevent the spray from washing into the cabin. It made the entrance and exit through the companionway an awkward operation, especially in big boots and bulky storm gear.

Soon Jonathan was back at the entrance, hands laden with food.

"Hand the stuff to me before you come out," Marshall said, reaching out to take the thermos and packet of sandwiches. "And remember to hang on."

"Careful," Robert said, resisting the urge to reach out a hand to his son.

Jonathan had just climbed up over the bottom slide and was out, when a sudden lurching movement of the boat made him lose his balance. With a yell he hurtled over the lifelines and Robert saw him make a futile attempt to grab a hold of them. Before his horrified eyes Jonathan plunged into the dark, surging waters.

Robert's reaction was instantaneous. He flung out the yellow horseshoe lifebuoy that was within his reach and was gratified to see that Jonathan managed to grasp it. The chemical flare attached to the lifebuoy lit up instantly and a moment later Robert was relieved to hear the sound of a shrill whistle above the storm. Jonathan had been able to locate the emergency whistle attached to his life vest and he blew on it, while sputtering and flailing, buffeted around by the waves.

"Olivia, keep an eye on the flare," Robert yelled. "Keep pointing to it so I'll know where he is. And don't lose him!"

"Marshall, stand by with the boat hook and heaving line!" he roared above the storm.

With a quick gybe he turned the sloop around and started the motor in readiness. Through all this, the horrible reality pounded in his brain. Jonathan was gone! He knew there was no possible way they could find him in the black night.

But despite this, Robert strained his vision, trying to pierce through the darkness with haunted eyes, trying to keep the bow pointed in the direction of Olivia's arm. The waves seemed mountainous. They tossed the boat high and the next moment sent it plummeting down into a trough. Desperately his eyes clung to the lifebuoy flare whenever it came into view on the crest of a wave. Through the storm he could hear Jonathan's whistle and Olivia's shouts of encouragement.

But then, to his horror, Olivia screamed in panic. "I can't see the flare! I've lost him! I've lost him!"

"Oh God," Robert moaned and then he lashed out

in tormented fury. "Damn it all! I told you to keep your eyes on that flare!"

"I did, Daddy! I tried!" Olivia sobbed. She leaned out over the lifelines to see better, but Robert grabbed the loop of her life vest and yanked her into the cockpit.

"Get back!" he shouted angrily. "I don't want to lose you, too!"

He held onto the useless tiller, simply trying to keep the boat from wallowing and rocking crazily. He had no idea in which direction he should steer. He had never in his life felt more helpless. Anguish tore through him. He had to find his son! He had to find him so he could tell him how much he loved him. Tell him how sorry he was for all the missed years and for all the grief he'd caused.

But now that chance was lost forever. Jonathan was gone.

Suddenly both Olivia and Marshall shot out their arms to point into the storm. The light had popped into view again!

"There he is! There he is!" Olivia screamed. "Jonathan! Jonathan! We're coming! Keep blowing the whistle! We're coming!"

"Stand by to haul him up," Robert shouted to Marshall, once more in command of himself and the boat. As though his own life depended on it, he kept his eyes on the light whenever it reappeared.

At last they came alongside Jonathan. Robert idled the motor and dropped the sails with lightning speed. He handed the tiller to Olivia.

"Just hold it steady into the waves," he commanded.

Marshall threw the heaving line to Jonathan, who grabbed a hold of it and hung on. At the same time she tried unsuccessfully to snag the bobbing loop of his life vest with the boat hook. Robert reached down with his hand to grab a hold of the loop and then struggled to pull up his son, who was so heavy in his waterlogged clothing that Marshall's help was needed to get him over the coaming.

When the ordeal was over Jonathan lay gasping on the cockpit seat. Robert fell to his knees beside him and his tears of relief flowed unchecked. He grasped his son in his arms and held him fiercely against his chest.

"Jonathan, Jonathan, please forgive me," he choked out brokenly. "I love you, son. I thought I'd lost you and would never have the chance to ask you to forgive me." He rocked Jonathan against him. "You're safe," he kept repeating, sobbing with relief, drawing reassurance from being able to hold his son. Alive.

And then he felt Jonathan's hand on his head, stroking it.

"Dad, I knew you'd find me," Jonathan said. "You always were the best."

Marshall saw the effect Jonathan's words had on Robert. He buried his head on Jonathan's chest and his shoulders heaved with sobs while Jonathan now rocked him in his arms.

After a while Robert raised his head and looked up at Marshall who stood beside them, hanging on to one of the stays for support. His face shone with happiness and to Marshall it was as though the sun had broken out in the middle of the dark storm. All the doubt and fear in her heart dissipated, replaced by a wonderful, glorious lightness she'd thought she would never feel again.

She place her hand on Robert's shoulder. "Better get Jonathan down and help him out of his wet clothes," she said gently. "I'll get him a hot drink from the thermos."

"Your mother's right, son. You're freezing," Robert said. "I'll take you below." But even then he seemed reluctant to release his son, and his arm remained around him protectively, as they both stood up, bracing themselves against the erratic movement of the boat.

It was only then that Robert became aware of Olivia, still sitting at the helm, clutching the tiller as had been his command. Tears streamed down her face, mingling with the rain.

"Honey, I'm sorry I left you there," Robert said. "You're doing a super job. Keep it up for just a while longer, sweetheart."

Olivia smiled, and gave her face a wipe with her wet sleeve. "I'm all right, Daddy. Just look after Jonathan."

Robert propelled Jonathan down into the cabin. Marshall followed and poured her son a brandy. Robert held the glass steady as Jonathan gulped down the powerful drink and coughed as the strong fumes caught his breath.

Marshall then poured mugs of coffee from a thermos for the men and two more for Olivia and herself. She turned to go up, but then turned back and gave a kiss to both Robert and Jonathan. Her two men, together at last.

During this time the sloop had been pitching aimlessly, buffeted by the wind and waves and lashed by the steady rain, with hapless Olivia holding onto the tiller with obviously no idea what she was supposed to be doing.

But as soon Robert returned to take command things were once more under control. He quickly raised the sails, checked the compass, and set the course toward their destination. And, with the sails pulling again, the movement of the boat became purposeful and a great deal more comfortable.

Exhausted by the shock of his ordeal Jonathan fell asleep, dry and cozy in his sleeping bag. He didn't awake when they entered Wingfield Basin and anchored in the calm waters of the harbour.

It was only the next day, toward noon, that Jonathan finally rose, and Olivia and Marshall both filled him in on what had transpired during the night.

"The storm went on and on and the thunder went away and then came back again," Olivia told him. "It was so frustrating. Just when you think it's over, it starts to rain and thunder all over again."

"The waves stayed high all night," Marshall said. "And I think they still are pretty big out there, though it's so calm here in the harbour."

"We were drenched to the skin, like we'd all gone overboard and not just you." Olivia continued. "Mommy stayed below with you. She said she wanted to make sure you were okay, but I think she just wanted to keep dry."

"I did not! I was as wet as you!" Marshall cried. "And I had to keep bringing you sandwiches and hot chocolate."

"It sure was a sweet feeling to see those buoys pointing the way to the harbour!" Olivia told Jonathan. "And when we came into the basin and everything was so calm and peaceful and the storm was behind us," she exhaled, "Wow! What a feeling. Relief with a capital R!"

"Now I know how sailors feel when they talk about a safe haven and a refuge from the storm," Marshall said. "It was like a miracle."

"Too bad I missed it. You should have woken me up," Jonathan said. "It sounds like a great experience."

"Listen, son, you'd already had a pretty great experience," Robert said.

He laughed with Jonathan, and the sound warmed Marshall's heart. Since last night she'd been bursting with joy as she replayed Jonathan's words in her head. She knew she would treasure them forever.

Chapter Twelve

They sailed into Tobermory in the late afternoon, under a brilliant blue sky, the gentle swells the only reminders of last night's storm.

"I hate to leave her without first getting her all scrubbed and tidy," Robert said to Olivia and Jonathan, who were finished packing their duffle bags and stood, ready to leave. "We'll stay for a while and clean up. Your mom's great with a rag and teak oil."

But as soon as they'd waved bye to the kids, Robert turned to Marshall. "Polishing be damned," he said. "There's something I have to say to you. Could you please put on some fresh coffee for us first?"

He sat down on the berth and as soon as the coffee was brewing, he indicated that she should sit down beside him. For a few minutes he just sat, hunched over, his elbows resting on his knees.

Marshall waited without a word.

"I've been thinking," Robert began hesitantly. "All the time we've been sailing back, I've been trying to imagine what you went through that night when I stayed out drinking and in your heart you were convinced I was dead." He frowned. "Isn't that coffee ready yet?"

Marshall poured each of them a mug and he took an eager gulp.

"Damn, this is hot!"

"Coffee usually is."

"I think I know how you felt," he went on, "because that's how I felt when Jonathan fell overboard. I didn't want to tell you, but I knew he was gone. In a storm like that, it's absolutely impossible to find anyone, so even though I kept telling you to keep an eye out for him, I knew it was useless. He was dead, or he would be in a few hours when the cold got to him, or he breathed water into his lungs. Yes, he was wearing a life jacket, but by the time the Coast Guard got a search going and found him on that huge lake—" He didn't finish but ran a hand across his eyes. "And my heart was aching because I knew he was a wonderful young man, and he was my son, and I would never have a chance to tell him how sorry I was, and that I loved him. He was gone and I cried and I cried. You didn't see because everything was wet anyhow."

Marshall was silent but her heart was pounding heavily in her breast.

"So I know that's probably kind of how you felt when in your heart you knew I was dead," Robert continued.

This was what she'd been hoping for all these years, that one day he would understand how she'd suffered that night. He would probably never understand how grievously wounded she'd been when she found out he'd been out drinking and hadn't bothered to let her know. But one day, when he had time to think about things some more, maybe he would realize why she couldn't take it any longer. Why she'd had to end it.

"I sat there today, steering and looking at you, and

I tried to imagine how I would feel if you didn't come home one night and there'd been an accident and you were dead. Just imagining that—" His eyes filled and he grinned bashfully, wiping them with his thumb. "Jeesh, just talking about it now breaks me up."

"It's okay." Marshall said and her eyes grew moist. She put out a hand to him, but he didn't take it.

"Let me finish before I turn into a blubbering idiot," Robert said. "About my drinking . . . I want to tell you that I really do understand that you can never trust me completely. But I'm okay with that. Hell, I can't even trust myself. But I want you to know that I'm going to try my damnest to stay sober. I'll join AA again, and I hope that'll help you feel a bit more secure about things. I don't know if it will, but I'm hoping, because—"

Robert paused and Marshall saw his Adam's apple working. "What I'm trying to say is that I realize I took your love for granted when I first came back into your life. I could tell you loved me and wanted me. That was easy to see—"

Marshall grimaced. "I'm that easy to read?"

Robert grinned. "Yes, you're that easy to read, because I remember how you looked when you were ready to make love." Then he became serious again. "I imagined we could just pick up where we left off. I know now that we couldn't, but Marshall, I love you more than I ever thought possible."

Now Robert took the hand she offered to him. "I know there's this alcoholism sickness that we can't just brush under the table, but I'd be eternally grateful if you'd take me back as your husband and let me show you how much you mean to me. I promise I'll do my damnest to make you happy. I know there are no guarantees in life, but . . ." He raised her hand to his lips and kissed the palm. "One thing I can guarantee is that I'll love you as long as I live."

Robert's words hit her with a flash of clarity and suddenly Marshall saw the future in a different light. There were no guarantees in life, he'd said, and she realized this was true, not just for his alcoholism, but for everything. She had no way of knowing if one day something might happen and she would find herself alone again. It might not be his alcoholism, but some illness that could take him away. But until that time she and Robert could love each other, and live every day together as if it were their last.

Because this day was all anyone ever had.

Marshall kissed the hand that held hers. "And I would be eternally grateful if you would take me back as your wife," she said. This was it. She was committing herself to a life with him, for as long as their life together would last.

Robert leaned back against the cushions. "Darling, you have no idea how happy you have just made me. When I heard Jonathan say that he knew I'd find him, and that I was the best, I thought I couldn't possibly be happier. But your words, they make me feel like I've just won gold at the Olympics!"

He pulled her close, and Marshall wondered how she could ever have thought Steve's arm had felt secure. She sighed with satisfaction as Robert held her firmly against him.

Marshall turned to look up at him and saw the fire in his eyes.

"And now for the prize," he murmured.

She knew this time there was no holding him back. And this time she didn't want to.

"Please?" With a groan Robert took her face in his hands and brought his lips fervently against hers.

Holding his hand, Marshall led him down into the cabin and lay down on the narrow berth against the wall.

"Should we pull it out wider?" Robert asked.

Marshall eyed him impishly. "Are you planning to sleep on top of me or beside me?"

"Top."

"Well, then . . .?"

Robert slipped off his shorts and stood before her, naked. And she feasted her eyes on his smooth, bronzed skin and well-toned muscles. He had already reached almost full erection and her body was reacting, deep inside.

"Are you going to undress me?" she asked, trying for a casual tone, but her voice cracked with need. "Or work around the clothes."

"We've done that before," he reminded her. "When necessary."

"True."

He came to the berth and knelt down on the floor beside it. She was wearing her light sleeveless dress, in preparation for the drive home. He now scrunched the hem in his hands and pulled it up to her waist, revealing her pink silky panties.

Marshall lay back, just wanting to feel. Wanting him to do whatever he wished to her, because she knew she would not be disappointed. He parted her legs slightly and first caressed the inside of her knees softly with his fingers, and then with his mouth. His lips continued up the inside of her thigh until he was kissing her through the panty.

She was already delirious with desire and strained

herself against him, opening herself up for more. The world moved under her.

He pulled the panty down and she helped by raising her hips and then he got onto the berth and she felt his weight on her, felt him between her legs. Where he belonged.

"Now where were we before the kids so rudely interrupted us yesterday?" he murmured and slipped inside her, filling her the way she knew he always could. But instead of giving her time to luxuriate in the feeling, he began to plunge into her with quick, deep thrusts.

The coupling was wanton and short, almost reckless, and she moaned and pushed herself up against him as the climax built inside her. She couldn't wait, and it was obvious from his wild, primitive rhythm, neither could he. Her release came, like the storm they had just been through, only more relentless and savage, and she bit into his shoulder to prevent herself from crying out. She could feel him tighten and he groaned her name as he came.

Breathless and spent they lay on the berth, Robert still on top supporting himself up on his elbows to ease his weight off her.

"Let's just call this foreplay," he said. "Next time I want to take it slow and easy and really adore you."

Marshall stretched deliciously. "I can't wait. But now we better head for home, because I still have some planning to do for school tomorrow."

"I guess that means I can't stay the night?" he asked with a droopy-dog look as he rolled off her. "Olivia thought it would be a good idea, remember?"

"I remember, but first I want to talk to her so she won't feel we're just ignoring her. After all, it's her home, too, and I want to make sure she's totally okay with you moving in with us." She wasn't going to confess that she would like nothing better, after this lovemaking, than for them to continue it tonight. In fact, she suspected she would find it difficult to concentrate on her schoolwork. "But I'm sure once we tell her about our plans, she'll be very happy about it," she added.

Robert kissed her. "I'll dream about it tonight."

"Why isn't Daddy here tonight?" Olivia asked.

It was Friday night and Robert often came to spend the evening. And if Olivia was at a friend's house— especially overnight—he would stay longer and they would have wonderful sex and talk about the future.

Robert was showing uncommon patience, letting her call the shots and giving her space to decide when she was ready. Marshall smiled. Maybe the fact that they were having sex made him more patient than he would normally have been.

"Your father went sailing with some old friends," she told Olivia. "He said he'll call when they're back at the marina."

She didn't tell Olivia that some of the "old friends" were men he'd gone sailing with years ago. Marshall hadn't said anything to him, but she couldn't help feeling uneasy that he still associated with them. She didn't know if they were heavy drinkers, but drinking certainly had been a big part of their routine in the past.

She worked on her lesson plans, and when she was done, she switched on the TV. Still feeling restless, she picked up a book she'd been reading, but had to put it down when she couldn't focus.

What was the matter with her? If Robert couldn't go sailing with whomever he wished, then there was no use even thinking about a future together. Just because in the past all sailing trips had ended with him coming home drunk, it didn't mean that this was going to happen now. She knew it was just her mind reacting in the old way. She knew that, so why was she then getting so nervous about this?

Olivia came to kiss her good night. "Daddy hasn't called yet?"

"No, he hasn't. They'll probably get in quite late. Maybe he won't call till tomorrow."

"Right." Olivia yawned loudly and turned to go up to her room.

At midnight Marshall went to bed but couldn't sleep. She wished Robert would have called by now. She turned on the bedside radio and found the weather station. Georgian Bay was infamous for its unpredictable winds and its dangerous rocky shoals, but tonight there were no heavy winds reported in the area, so she could stop worrying about that. Besides, she knew Robert was an excellent sailor. Hadn't he more than proven himself during the storm? She had nothing to worry about.

By two o'clock she still hadn't fallen asleep. Surely he couldn't possibly have stayed out drinking all night with his sailing buddies. Marshall pulled the duvet over her head and tried to prevent her mind from dwelling on that thought, but there was nothing she could do to keep the memories of that horrible night long ago from invading her brain.

Damn, damn, damn! She flung the covers aside and got up. In the kitchen she fixed herself some hot chocolate and then plunked herself into the big armchair in the family room to watch TV. She found an old movie playing on the all-night movie channel and smiled as she remembered how Jonathan had joked in the park about her watching black and white silent films.

Yes, Jonathan and Robert were getting along so well now. They had even been to a baseball game and Marshall couldn't have been happier. The two men she loved most in the world were friends. More than friends—they were father and son.

Robert would never jeopardize that.

Would he? Alcoholics were unpredictable. You could never trust them. Marshall squirmed in the armchair and shivered. If those sailing buddies had started to drink—which was very possible—would Robert have been able to resist joining in? He'd started going to AA, just as he'd promised, but so far had only been to a couple of meetings.

It wasn't until the rays of the morning sun beamed in through the windows and hit her eyes that Marshall awoke and realized she'd fallen asleep. An old Henry Fonda western was playing on TV and she was still curled up in the armchair, wrapped in a blanket.

Just then the phone rang and Marshall quickly grabbed it.

"Good morning, sweetheart," came Robert's cheerful voice. "I hope I didn't wake you, but I wanted to call as soon as we got in."

"How come you just got in now?" Fear nagged at her heart.

"Would you believe, there's no reception out on the lake. Each of us had a phone and we couldn't even make one lousy phone call."

"Hmm." His answer sounded almost too glib.

"What? You don't believe me?"

"I didn't say that." But she had thought of it.

"And the wind died down," he went on. "We were sitting in a total calm. And on top of no phone reception, and no wind, the stupid diesel wouldn't start. Talk about Murphy's Law."

Sure, blame Murphy. He was laying it on a bit too thick to be real.

"I'll be there shortly," Robert said. "Make me a pot of coffee. Maybe even a bit of breakfast?"

"Okay." Her voice wasn't welcoming.

Two hours later the doorbell rang and Marshall could hear Olivia's chipper voice at the door.

"Good morning, Daddy! How was the sail? Boy, you look terrible, like you've been up all night or something. Don't smell so great either."

Robert laughed. "Thanks, honey."

"I'll go jump in the shower," Olivia said. "And then I'll come and have some breakfast with you."

Marshall didn't go to greet him at the door. She stayed in the kitchen, sitting by the counter on a bar stool with her coffee, trying with difficulty to swallow a piece of dry toast.

Robert came in but hesitated, obviously not sure of his welcome. "Good morning," he said. "I think?"

Marshall refused to look up.

"You're mad because I didn't call you last night? But I already told you why." He got on a bar stool beside her.

Marshall stole a sidelong glance at him. She pinched her lips in a tight line, not wanting to smell the alcohol on him.

Robert was starting to get the message. "Marshall, what the hell's the matter?"

He was getting annoyed. But so was she. In fact, she was beyond annoyed, reaching for furious. "Have you looked at yourself in a mirror lately?" she snapped.

"Wha-at?" He went over to the hall mirror and she heard him whistle. "Wow! No wonder Olivia said I looked terrible. I rushed right over and didn't even stop at my hotel room to shower. I'm sorry, darling, but I didn't think my looks would affect you like this."

She had to remain totally cool. Calm. "To me you look exactly like you've been boozing." There. The words were out. No taking them back now.

Robert appeared at the doorway. To her surprise he looked incredulous rather than angry. "You really think that?" His voice sounded disappointed.

"Well . . ."

He came closer and she could only detect the usual boat smells on his clothes.

"I wasn't drinking."

She knew that now and guilt filled her. She had done it again. Just like at the party, when she hadn't trusted him and had unfairly accused him. Only this time she'd done it to his face. Again, she had caused herself totally unnecessary grief.

She couldn't blame him if he told her he couldn't tolerate living with someone who didn't trust him, someone who was always suspicious of his actions.

Robert sat down at the kitchen table. "You know," he began and then swallowed, hesitating. "I can see how you might have worried and thought I was drinking. But I honestly didn't expect you to get this upset." He sat frowning, fingering the placemat. "I don't know . . ."

Marshall felt a streak of fear course through her. As far as she was concerned, there was no doubt in her mind that she wanted to live with him for the rest of her life. But could she trust herself not to freak out every time something looked suspicious? Like at the party, or now, when he'd gone sailing with his old buddies? Both times it had turned out she was wrong, and had worked herself into a panic for no reason.

But could Robert put up with that? Would he reconsider their plans for a future together? How many times would she hurt him with her accusations before she could unlearn this conditioned response that came from years of having lived with those situations? Could he live with a wife who might fly off the handle at the slightest suspicion of drinking on his part?

Marshall wanted him to know exactly what he would be getting into if he married her.

"I've been thinking," she began hesitantly, knowing she could be signing the death warrant for their life together. "I know that being suspicious and getting angry with you is a conditioned response on my part. I just react to something automatically, without giving you a chance to explain yourself. Like if I see you with a glass of wine I get all tense and upset and think you're going to fall off the wagon."

"If you saw me with a glass of wine, I think it would be pretty reasonable for you to assume I'm falling off the wagon," Robert said.

"Yes, but at the party you were just getting the wine for me," she explained. "Remember?"

Robert burst out laughing. "Oh my God! You thought I was going to drink it?"

"Yes. And I'm ashamed to admit I was totally freaking out about it."

"Darling, I'm so sorry. I was just trying to be helpful. I didn't mean to upset you."

Marshall was surprised and relieved he wasn't angry at her confession. "I made *myself* upset. I should have waited to see what it was all about before I flipped. And now, when you went sailing with your old buddies, I felt anxious and worried that you might start to drink with them." She didn't want to go on, but forced herself to spit it all out. "When you called with your many explanations, I didn't wait to see if they were true. I just figured you were making up a bunch of incredible, slick excuses. I went by what always happened before—you go sailing, you come home drunk. Period." She stopped to take a deep breath. "I'm so sorry, but I can't promise it won't happen again. After all those years, it seems that kind of reaction is ingrained in me."

Robert reached for her hand and held it against his heart. "It's my job, then, to make sure I behave in such a way that you can learn to trust me. I deserve your distrust after all the agony I put you through. I can't say I like being accused wrongly, but I can't complain about it, either, because I brought it on myself."

Marshall felt his heart beating under her palm. "And I promise I'm going to try my very best to move forward and learn to deal with my insecurities."

He pulled her close and kissed her neck, sending delicious shivers through her. "Now, about that breakfast. . .?"

Marshall slipped out of his embrace. "First things first." The feeling of relief and happiness made her almost fly up the stairs. From her jewelry box in her bedroom she took out two rings and brought them down into the kitchen.

Robert sat, looking puzzled. But when she handed the rings to him his face lit up, for they were the same rings he had given her almost thirty years ago. He slipped the plain gold ring into the pocket of his jeans. Then, dropping down on one knee, he held the diamond up to her. "Marshall, will you marry me?"

She smiled. "I already said I would, remember?"

"Just checking to make sure you haven't changed your mind." He got up and slipped the diamond on her finger where it had always belonged, and then he kissed it.

"But will *you* marry *me*?" Marshall asked.

Robert gave her one of those sexy smiles that still had the same effect on her after all these years. It still made her want to kiss him. So she did.

"Okay, I'll marry you," he said. "If you make me that breakfast."

Marshall gave him another kiss, and then proceeded to scramble him a couple of eggs.

About Karen Rossi

Karen Rossi (the pen name of Kaarina Brooks) has been a romantic since she was a child. She and her sister had their own "publishing company" and wrote about love-struck princes and princesses.

Today she writes grown-up romances where modern-day "princes and princesses" go through heart-wrenching relationship struggles before reaching their happily ever after.

She now also has a real publishing company, Wisteria Publications. Besides romances, she also publishes kids' books and non-fiction works, such as a cook book.

She lives in Southern Ontario with her husband and kitty-cat, Lilly.

www.wisteriapublications.com
brooks.kaarina@gmail.com